Praise

The Cost of Lunch, Etc.

With uncompromising emotional intensity, Piercy captures the complex female experience in her debut short story collection. Powerful in scope, the collection feels driven by an idea rather than a story, demonstrating Piercy's understanding of how social constructs evolve in deeply personal ways.
—*Publishers Weekly*

Piercy's latest short stories focus, as do her many novels, poetry collections, and earlier stories, on powerful female characters—women who are not always right, or sympathetic, or admirable, but definitely strong. Piercy homes in on her characters, mixing just the right amount of humor into her always insightful take on imperfect human relationships, in their many guises.

—*Booklist*

In short stories, the reader has only a few pages to identify with the protagonist. This means that effective short stories require strong characters, concise plots, and memorable settings. It also means that it can be difficult for a novelist to make the shift to short fiction. Happily, Marge Piercy has succeeded admirably with the twenty well-crafted tales in *The Cost of Lunch, Etc.*, her first short story collection. As in poetry, short fiction involves working within a limited space, and Piercy uses the skills she has earned as a poet to craft rich, succinct stories with quirky characters and layered imagery.
—*Rain Taxi*

Marge Piercy is a great poet and this is clearly evident in the way she handles words. This is her first collection of short stories (although drawn from the work of a number of years) but the same economy of phrase, depth of emotion and touch of astringency you find in her poetry is here...

These stories bear the hallmark of the '70s feminist movement—not in terms of setting, there are stories set up to today—but in terms of the emotional tenet and confessional nature of the collection. Men do not on the whole come out of the stories very well but you do get to meet an amazing caste of vulnerable, gritty and generally fabulous women of all ages.

Many of the stories are funny, a few shocking, all are interesting and incredibly well-told. For a journey into the feminine psyche it is unparalleled.

—*We Love This Book*

These stories entrance and satisfy at the highest level. I recently read an article that described the initial screening for a new movie release. At the end, a young audience member stands and says, "You've just captured my life." That's just what Piercy does—and what a good short story can do—by capturing a quick-flash photo illuminating some act or thought that rings true in our own personal experience.

—*Barnstable Patriot*

The Cost of
Lunch, Etc.

Other books by Marge Piercy

POETRY

Made in Detroit

The Hunger Moon: New & Selected Poems, 1980–2010

The Crooked Inheritance

Colors Passing Through Us

The Art of Blessing the Day

What Are Big Girls Made Of?

Available Light

Stone, Paper, Knife

The Moon Is Always Female

Living in the Open

Hard Loving

Breaking Camp

Early Grrrl

Mars and Her Children

My Mother's Body

Circles on the Water (Selected Poems)

The Twelve-Spoked Wheel Flashing

To Be of Use

4-Telling (*with Bob Hershon, Emmett Jarrett and Dick Lourie*)

NOVELS

Sex Wars

The Third Child

Three Women

Going Down Fast

The Longings of Women

Summer People

Fly Away Home

Vida

Woman on the Edge of Time

Small Changes

Storm Tide (*with Ira Wood*)

City of Darkness, City of Light

He, She and It

Gone to Soldiers

Braided Lives

The High Cost of Living

Dance the Eagle to Sleep

OTHER

My Life, My Body

Pesach for the Rest of Us

So You Want to Write: How to Master the Craft of Writing

Fiction and the Personal Narrative (*with Ira Wood*), 1st & 2nd editions

The Last White Class: A Play (*with Ira Wood*)

Sleeping with Cats: A Memoir

Parti-Colored Blocks for a Quilt: Essays

Early Ripening: American Women's Poetry Now

The Cost of Lunch, Etc.

Marge Piercy

The Cost of Lunch, Etc.
Short stories by Marge Piercy

Acknowledgments
"The Cost of Lunch, Etc.," *Aphra*. "Saving Mother from Herself," *Ms. Magazine*.
"Going over Jordan," *Transatlantic Review*. "Somebody Who Understands You,"
Moving Out. "Do You Love Me?" *The Second Wave*. "The Retreat," *Provincetown
Poets*. "The Border," *Crossroads*. "Ring around the Kleinbottle," *Fifth Wednesday*.
"The Shrine," *december*. "The Easy Arrangement," published in an earlier form
as "Professor Wrong" in *Mr. Wrong: Real-Life Stories about the Men We Used to
Love*. "Fog," *Paterson Literary Review*. "What and When I Promised," *Blue Lyra
Review*. "Little Sister, Cat and Mouse," *The Second Wave*. "I Wasn't Losing My
Mind," published in an earlier form as "The Necklace" in *What My Mother
Gave Me: Thirty-one Women on the Gifts That Mattered Most*. "The Secret of My
Marriage," *Jewish Women's Annual*.

ISBN: 978-1-62963-125-7
Library of Congress Control Number: 2015930895

Cover by John Yates / www.stealworks.com
Interior design by briandesign

10 9 8 7 6 5 4 3 2 1

PM Press
PO Box 23912
Oakland, CA 94623
www.pmpress.org

Printed in the USA by the Employee Owners of Thomson-Shore
in Dexter, Michigan.
www.thomsonshore.com

Contents

Introduction

These short stories were written over decades; of course the older ones were revised a little or a lot for this collection. At least half of them were written after the book contract was signed. Before being approached for this book, I had not worked in this genre for years. I discovered that, at this point in my life, I not only enjoy writing short stories but prefer them to novels. When the book went to press, I didn't stop writing them. Two of the new ones are included in this paperback.

I have used the short story form mostly to explore the lives of women. Some of the stories are autobiographical, more or less, but don't assume that the ones written in the first person are and the ones written in the third person aren't. That doesn't follow. Sometimes a character has a strong voice, like the woman in "Saving Mother from Herself." Such a character wants the first person and may even directly address the reader. Sometimes to gain perspective on something painful or difficult in a writer's life, the third person helps. Sometimes a story is almost an anecdote and the first person feels natural.

The protagonists range in age from children ("She's Dying, He Said") to adolescents ("Crossing over Jordan," "Somebody Who Understands You") to middle age ("What the Arbor Said") and old ladies ("Fog"), with just about every part of lives in between. Some protagonists are well-off, many are not. Some are political, as in "The Border," and some could care less, as in "The Shrine." Some are concerned with love, some with marriage, some with money, some with political choices, some with friendship, some with religion, some with health, some with a writer's life or choices.

Don't assume that a story set in the '70s was written before a story set now. I know I gave that away in the story "Do You Love Me?" when I had the protagonist drag a suitcase on wheels. That's a stupid anachronism, as there were no suitcases on wheels in the era when the story is set. That got by me until after the book was published and I was reading the story at the Newport Literary Festival and, boing! I heard my mistake too late to change it.

There's a range of styles, as some readers have noticed and seemed surprised at. I try to adjust style to character and story. Some stories take a more literary style and others demand to be cast in a casual-seeming tone that pretends to be conversational, as in "I Had a Friend." Some want images and a succinct style like "The Retreat."

Writing a short story feels to me midway between writing a poem and writing a novel. Almost every novel has some passages any particular reader may decide to skip; a short story has to grab your attention and hold it all the way through, like a poem. Nothing superfluous can stay. That too is like a poem, but not as extremely so. Every word in a poem is deliberated again and again as I'm working. Short stories are not for me quite so dogged, although some are close enough.

Some stories read aloud better than others, but I think most of them work if you want to perform them. I hope mostly that you will enjoy visiting the lives of these women and an occasional man and come away with something of value. I hope I'll write many short stories after this group and that you may like them.

Marge Piercy
March 2015

The Cost of Lunch, Etc.

Circa 1970

When the knocking came, Maud was taking a sponge bath.

Grabbing the sheet from the daybed she stuck her head out. One of the old men from the first floor stood there looking sore. "You got a phone call—why don't you come down to the phone when I call? All the way up here on account of you don't listen . . ."

Clutching the sheet she ran for the upstairs extension, right across from the john. Hearing Duncan's voice she was sure it was all off. "Duncan, what is it? He can't make it? He won't meet me?"

"Of course, Maud, don't get excited. Didn't I tell you it's all arranged?" His voice playing cool and dependable. "Just a little change of plans. First, we're not meeting at my place . . ."

"Oh." Goodbye to his wife's potato salad, the sesame crackers and cheeses—Port Salut, Roquefort, Camembert. All day she had been figuring the odds on salami, slicing those virgin cheeses. Gorgonzola, Gouda, Brie.

"Bill wants to meet us in town, at the Low Blow. There's a jazz man he wants to hear." The familiarity of the first name hung on the telephone wire as if with clothespins.

She had an urge to add the last name. The lumpy old man from downstairs had not hung up. He wouldn't know who

W. Saltzman was. They hated her in the roominghouse, her and the two still sexual men up on three: said they were noisy, said they used the phone too much. Doors opened eye-wide behind her in the halls, but when she spoke to them, the old men answered with suspiciously pursed lips if at all. Duncan was warning briskly that she not be late. He would pick her up—he and the wife, chuckle. Damp under the sheet she ran for her room. Duncan was eager to fuck her, would like to set up an extracurricular lay on Fridays after his last class. He taught at the college but lived in a house adorned with oriental carpets in an older suburb. With lumbering suaveness he tried to nudge her guilty for lunches at his expense in an off-campus Italian restaurant. Often he spoke of his friendship with the poet W. Saltzman, discovering in her work even more influence than there was, quoting the great man on trivial occasions. Introducing Saltzman was an attempt to net her in obligation: rubbing herself dry, she grinned.

Rhoda, his wife, was an excellent cook. Rhoda: chicken gently sautéed in white-wine sauce, roast sesame lamb, avocado salad. She would move in, if Rhoda would cook for her. But Duncan was a beefy milk-fed professor; from dead men's bones he ground plastic bread. He was so sure she was his proper prey, a rootless, nameless arty girl half nuts and outside the pale: because it never, never occurred to him that she might be a real writer.

She put on her good dress—the shade of blue was good, anyhow. The refrigerator held about a glass of milk and something in a napkin. She babysat occasionally for a couple she'd known during her stint teaching at the college. Besides baby food, she'd turned up maraschino cherries, cocktail onions and half a box of animal crackers.

She had consumed the cherries and onions and carried off the box.

She poured out a little milk and sat slowly chewing the crackers, eating each animal paw by paw and the head last.

She crossed to the john then. The light was on, the door ajar. The toilet was filled to the brim, splashing over to puddle the floor.

Lazily, like a carp in the bowl, a long cigar-brown turd floated. She backed out.

She had as landlady an ex-inmate of Treblinka. She would go down tomorrow to complain, and Mrs. Goldman would show her tattoo: Mr. Goldman and the little Goldmen long since ashes. Mrs. Goldman would assure her she was lucky to be in the United States and alive. She would retreat apologizing. Nothing was commensurate, and the plumbing broke every two weeks. Mrs. Goldman would hint she was flushing Tampax down the toilet, and she would deny it. Mrs. Goldman would bat her large weak eyes in disbelief. She and Mrs. Goldman would continue the argument as she backed up the staircase. Then Mrs. Goldman would utter a few Yiddish curses for women of loose morals and retire, slamming her door. Maud would piss in the sink as she did now, then run over to the college whenever possible. The college, where she had taught until replaced by a PhD, who was equally needy and would be equally badly paid, had useful facilities.

She reread the poems she had gone through five times. Saltzman could tell her where to send stuff, give her introductions, even help her find a job, point her out to editors, tell her how to get a book published. He was power. Besides it was getting to be winter. Though he was not her only literary pa, surely he would not mind the other influences. He was the local celebrity and everybody claimed to know him or his ex-girlfriend or his dentist. Imagining this meeting had soothed her to sleep bitter nights. She felt she was stumbling in darkness about to come round a corner into blinding light and be—not consumed but transfigured. Someday she would make it, why not now? She had to: how else could she survive?

The buzzer rasped. She jumped up. Turned, grabbed the envelope of poems. Saw herself in the bar bearing down on him poems in hand. She took out the bottom three, her cream, shoved them in her purse. Just happened to have on me. Well, shit, he could ask. Shrugging on her mouton coat. Going slowly down she felt the weight of the coat. It had been Sandy's. A year in the state hatch, insulin, electric shock and hydrotherapy had dulled her, but not enough. When Mrs. Gross decided Sandy was getting too wild and must be put away again, Sandy went up on the apartment house roof and jumped. She saw Sandy's long gentle face, her tea-brown hair, her freckled hands with the chewed nails, so vividly she could not take in Duncan. Docilely she followed him to the small Mercedes and got in back.

"What, Rhoda?" Maud came back into the present. "Oh, Harry the Tailor got robbed. No, they didn't smash the window when they robbed him, it was a man and a woman and they cut him up." She sat with head ducked, assuming Sandy's old position with hands knit, foot tapping shyly. Dead, stone dead. "No, some kids smashed the window, after." Mrs. Gross had acted funny when she gave her the coat. Maud had not wanted a fur coat—she thought they were gross, wearing the skin of some poor dead animal, but she did need a coat. Further, she felt she had a right to Sandy's things. What she wanted was Sandy's books, but Mrs. Gross brought out the coat. Mrs. Gross kept talking about how much she had paid for it, what good condition it was in, how little Sandy had worn it, till Maud had taken it to please her. She sat up, her knuckles bumping her teeth. Mrs. Gross had wanted her to pay for the coat. Then she began to laugh, covering her mouth so they would not hear.

Rhoda was sitting turned from Duncan. Her coat had a high fur collar, her reddish hair was done up in smooth whorls, and she radiated a faint smell of hair spray and spicy perfume. Rhoda did not like her because she was young, single and therefore presumably scheming. She and Rhoda were always talking in oblique boring sideways conversations. If they were to talk straight out:

RHODA: See my house! See my pretty things! They cost a lot! See how expensive I am.

MAUD: If you can't get out the door, have you tried the window?

RHODA: See my man. No Trespassing! Keep Off the Grass!

MAUD: It's only lunch I want. I swear it'll never happen while I'm conscious.

Duncan was of middle height but he sat tall: the Man behind the Desk. A dark blond thirty-eight, his jaw was square and he thrust it forward like a girl proud of her bosom. "Did you call Julie Norman about the seventeenth? I want her at the party."

"Duncan, I hardly know her," Rhoda whined.

"What do you mean, you don't know her? What do you do at those meetings?"

"You know what I mean." Rhoda's neck arched from the collar, angry goose neck stretching. "She won't remember me."

"Well, make her remember. Doesn't Susan play with her kid?"

"Let's leave Susan out of this."

"Out of what?" Duncan reared back from the wheel. "Can't you make a simple phone call?"

William Saltzman (Bill, Duncan had called him: hello, Bill, help!) made and broke reputations. His earlier poems were in the newer college anthologies. He had put out a paperback of younger poets, and why not me, dear god. Would he be gay? He was supposed to have had that affair with a woman anthropologist. Besides, his poems were full of breasts. She reached down the neck of her dress and jerked the bra straps tighter. Made a languorous face of surrender and giggled in disgust.

"There's the Low Blow." She leaned over Rhoda's shoulder to point.

"Yes, love, but do you think I can check the car with the hat girl?

The dashboard clock read five to nine. Her stomach dropped.

"There's a parking lot," Rhoda sang out.

"We're paying through the nose for a sitter. Hold on. Plenty of on-street parking."

They passed the Low Blow again. If it were like other jazz spots there would be nothing to eat. The rock music she heard with her last man never came there. Maybe afterward sandwiches, roast beef or pastrami. The clock hand slipped down from nine. "Maybe he won't wait, Duncan, if we're late."

"What do you think he'll do, go home? He'll be there." Around the block again past Nail It, past the Hoochie Mama All Night Hairdressers, past the Low Blow and Orvieto's pizzeria and Ron's Ale House and around the other corner. She sank back, cradling her cheek in Sandy's coat. Open the door and make a break for it. "There's somebody pulling out!" she yelled. He jammed on the brakes and backed into position, ignoring a Cadillac leaning on its horn.

"See," he said, expansive on the sidewalk with an arm guiding each woman, "Why pay a bundle? A little patience. Keep cool."

She dodged free of Duncan's arm entering and shrank behind him. What was the use, he wouldn't like her stuff. He'd say it was too female, too wet, too emotional, the way her own professors had. He must have his own protégées.

Duncan got tense, solider. "There he is."

"Where? Which one?" From behind she poked his arm.

"By the bar, talking with that big African American fellow."

Peeking around him, she studied W. Saltzman. Over loose and baggy Army fatigues he wore what had been a good leather jacket lined with fleece. He ought to feel hot in almost steamy room. He was tall with a gaunt face, a short kinky mustard yellow beard streaked with gray and a paunch sloping somewhat over his pants. His gaze on them, when finally he ended the conversation and waved them over, was cold and cat green.

She thought him a fine-looking man, because he was W. Saltzman and she knew his poems backwards, and because his cheeks and forehead were textured like weathered bark, and also because he had a satyr's paunch and must like food. But his eyes were cold as the sidewalks outside. Shuffling behind came a man his age and seedier, broader built, with a ruddy face, strong white hair and a knowing grin. Saltzman left the bar at a slow deliberate amble, looked at Duncan's outstretched hand for a moment, touched it.

Duncan said nervously, "How are you making it?"

W. Saltzman grunted. He said hello to Rhoda, looked then at Maud, was introduced. "We need a table, Ed," he said to the person who asked how many of them there were.

"Sure, Willy, right up front." They hung back in brief conversation. The table was tiny and near the small stage. Saltzman and his friend, still unintroduced, sat on one side, and the three of them huddled on the other. The set was starting.

"Uh, Bill," Duncan began.

Saltzman looked at Duncan with his eyelids lowered and then raised in disbelief. He motioned they should listen. The first round of drinks was on the house: Saltzman was known here. The second Duncan bought. The bourbon hurt her stomach. The tenor sax was a name she had heard, though she had thought him dead: a contemporary of Charlie Parker. She listened conscientiously, conscientiously not looking at Saltzman. Her hands sweated cold.

Saltzman offered a cigarette. She fumbled. Politely he lit it. The sound was dull, finally. The music said little to her, and after a while she was not listening but daydreaming about her next-to-last man, about getting published and getting laid and getting fed and keeping warm. She was drowsy and the music lulled her.

Duncan asked, "What's that smell?"

She felt a stab on her thigh. "Oh, shit." A hot ash had fallen from her cigarette and burnt through the dress. She brushed at it.

"What's wrong?" Saltzman looked halfway interested.

"Nothing, nothing really." Her face heated.

The waitress in short shorts brought another round and, after a longish pause, Duncan again paid. Fixing her gaze on Saltzman's mustard beard she willed him to notice her, to speak. At last when the set finished, he did, asking gently, "What do you do with yourself?"

Hadn't Duncan explained? "For a job you mean? I was teaching, and then—"

He nodded and leaned back as if his curiosity were satisfied. Quickly she added the important part. "But that's just what I do to support it, you know. I mean, I write poems."

His face shrank. Very quietly he mumbled, "Fuck."

His friend said cheerfully, "Everybody's doing it, doing it, doing it. They think it's poetry, but it's snot."

Her words lay on the table like a fat turd. For a moment she hated him. Did he think he would be the last poet? Duncan, the bastard, had said nothing. Produced her as random female.

Saltzman turned to him. "That workshop, how about it? I expected to hear by now. Is it coming off?"

The friend was staring at Duncan with shrewd assessment. Duncan furrowed his brow. "Arrangements take time. Departments of English grind exceedingly slowly and grind exceedingly fine. I'm pushing for it, every chance I get."

"Eh." The friend's mouth sagged. He shrugged his disbelief.

"I have to know soon. Other things depend on it."

"Like he has to pay the rent." His friend smirked. "And eat sometimes. Poets pay rent too. Ask the little lady."

"I'm trying to get a decision," Duncan said. "I'm trying to put it through. But you know how encrusted with tradition—

"Out on the west coast I had twelve readings in two weeks, including a couple of lectures."

"Kids were standing up outside wanting to hear him," the friend said. "Crowds of college kids."

"By the way, Saturday the seventeenth we're having a sort of pre-holiday thing. Wassail bowl and all, right, Rhoda? Most of the department will be there and the boys from the press, and we'd sure like to see you. And your friend too," he added weakly, but the tone of the invitation was confident.

Saltzman's old tomcat eyes went opaque. Duncan was putting it on the line. Even if Saltzman went, he wouldn't know if Duncan could or would arrange the workshop. Cf. her vague feeling that Duncan could have saved her job. "Sounds fine," said Saltzman. "I'll let you know. I'm spending the holidays in New York, and I don't know when I'm leaving."

The friend did not reply. Rattling the ice in her glass Rhoda came alive to ask, "Don't think I caught your name?"

"Charlie Roach," he said, inclining his head.

"He's one of the West Side roaches," Saltzman said and caught Maud's gaze as she smiled. She had given up. She pitied him with his grizzled beard and still needing Duncan.

Rhoda was being social. "And what do you do?" her voice slurred from rapid drinking.

Charlie grinned. His teeth were stained and worn down in his ruddy face. "Anything, Ma'am."

"Charlie's a true fan of the golden rule, though he likes to operate a little ahead of the beat."

Rhoda was flustered, as designed, but Duncan was enjoying the show. They couldn't shock him if they slit their gullets on his tweeds. Saltzman lolled back, withdrawn. She remembered the poems in her purse and bowed her head, fingering the cigarette burn that had marred her dress.

They were leaving. As they passed the bar, guys here and there slapped Saltzman's shoulder. On the sidewalk he halted, turned. For a moment he stared at her and she stared back. His eyes, ice green, were glacial crevasses, his mouth curled in a perhaps amused smile.

The eyes said he was bored sick with women wanting to fuck his name, with men wanting to suck his talent: he'd been used and used like an old toothpaste tube, he was well chewed. She looked back posturing, can't you see my ineffable Name, I'm as real as you but you only wanted a young girl to chew on tonight: your mistake, Willy, I'm good and you won't get into my biography for saving me, so there!

Following Duncan and Rhoda to the car she said hopefully, "Damn, I'm starving," but nobody answered. In the back seat she huddled into Sandy's coat. The first time she wore it she had found old Kleenexes in the pocket and unable to have preserved Sandy, preserved them. Then she caught a cold.

Not that long ago she had brooded over slitting her wrists: she felt ashamed. There were years, years yet of inventive tortures and deprivations, of hollow victories and bloody defeats. She no longer felt sorry for Saltzman. She would wear the same face. The worst that could happen then might be to meet a kid who had eaten her books and survived.

As for Duncan she could no longer afford his lasagna: she perceived he was her natural predator. The system supported him, and he supported the system. In any attempt to make a deal, he was more powerful than she and would prevail.

Saving Mother from Herself

My daughter Suzie and my brother Adam really got after me about what they called my hoarding. I live alone. My husband died when he was just fifty-eight of one of those heart attacks that hit without warning. He was playing golf— something he enjoyed but was never much good at—with another dentist and two podiatrists on the Wednesday when he just keeled over on the fifth hole trying to bang his way out of a sand trap. At first they thought he was kidding them. I was only fifty then.

I continued working, of course. I was a paralegal for thirty years in a small law office that did mostly real estate, wills and probate and small business stuff. I was really as much a secretary as a paralegal, if I'm honest. But it wasn't taxing. I liked the two men I worked for and it paid decently, a middling middle class wage, you might say. Four years ago, I retired. Actually they retired and closed the office, and at fifty-nine, I wasn't about to get hired to do anything better than greeting folks at Wal-Marts or bagging at the supermarket.

I had the insurance from Walt. I'd put it in CDs like my boss recommended. I had Walt's social security, which was better than mine would have been. I was okay. The mortgage on our house we paid off decades ago. It was the same house where I raised Suzie and my son Brady. Brady's out in

Arizona, so I only see him maybe every couple of years when he sends me tickets to fly out there. The last time was for my granddaughter Olivia's wedding. A very nice affair that must have set him back I can't imagine how much. Olivia's pregnant now, he tells me. I'll be a great grandmother before I can take that in. Amazing. Makes me feel ninety.

Suzie tried to get me to move into an apartment, but why? I'm used to this house. I know my neighbors and they know me. We don't hang out together, but we keep on eye on each other's property and have a friendly chat over the fence now and then. I have a nice little garden out back and a two-car garage. This house has three bedrooms so I have plenty of room for my things. That's what Suzie and Adam object to, as if there's something wrong with liking bargains and pretty things and useful things other people throw away. If you ask me, people discard too many items nowadays. I feel sorry when I see a perfectly good lamp or glassware or a rug that's still usable or even a flowerpot sitting in a dumpster or out on the street waiting for the pickup to be taken to the landfill. So I bring them home. I know I'll get some use out of them by and by. And books and magazines. Perfectly fine to read. And VCR tapes. At garage sales I can always find something interesting. When you live alone, you appreciate entertainment. I always have the TV on even when I'm reading. It's company. I like to keep up with the news and a few of my favorite programs, but mostly I appreciate hearing another human voice.

So I collected. Who cares except my busybody daughter and then she enlisted my older brother, who always used to try to boss me around before I married. He and his wife, Liz. She gives me a pain in the you-know-where. She seems to feel superior that she never worked. So she stayed home and raised two children. Big deal. I worked and raised two children and they turned out just fine. She always has her hair done and her nails too. As if at our age, anybody gives a damn, excuse my language, what her nails look like and if they're pink or red or purple. I'm too busy to fuss about my nails. Long red talons would never survive one of my scouting trips, collecting the wonderful stuff people discard. Besides, until Suzie butted in, Liz and Adam had no idea about my hobby. We always met in a restaurant (they paid). Liz had no desire to come by my house, and I have even less of a desire to visit them. I'd visited once and everything was so tidy and white and black I kept being afraid I'd spill coffee on that huge white couch as big as a boat. Adam and I never did have much in common.

So what if I filled up the dining room with my finds and the spare bedrooms and the hall that leads to them and half the living room. Who am I about to dine with, anyhow? What do I need spare bedrooms for? In the living room I store my reading material and VCR tapes and some extra VCRs people threw away. You can't buy a simple VCR any longer, and I keep about a dozen spares for when they go on the fritz. I'm always watching for them because I have a library of almost a thousand perfectly good tapes I can watch whenever I choose. My daughter calls it a mess, but I have them all cataloged. Just ask me. I can pull out any show I want, great old movies, some I saw and loved, others I never got a chance to see. Going to the movies used to be cheap, but now it's too rich for my purse. Why would I need to go to the movies anyhow with people nowadays being so rude and talking all through the movie and yakking on their cell phones? I have enough movies so I can see one whenever I choose. Now isn't that luxury? Every tape is catalogued. I have an old file cabinet I found behind the office building on 8th Street and in it every single book and magazine and VCR tape is listed, so I can pull out what I want. It may look a junkyard to Suzie, but it just plain isn't—or rather wasn't.

It isn't like Suzie is over here much. She likes to call me every couple of weeks and complain. I only hear from

Brady when he has something to boast about or wants to fly me down there for some event where a grandmother is welcome as some kind of certification of family. So he has his life, Suzie has hers and by the way, I also have mine.

I was just going along living my life happy as could be, collecting and sorting and cataloging, collecting and storing all the useful things I might need later on. I'm not Bill Gates (you didn't think I'd know who he was, but I saw a documentary on him, one of my tapes) so why should I ever have to buy what I can get free? Chairs, tables, lamps, cabinets, nice ornamental stuff like this stuffed owl I found—where else would I ever get a fine creature like Roscoe? Some people collect art or even stupid things like license plates or baseball cards, and nobody calls the feds on them. What's wrong with collecting useful things, I ask you? I feel bad for them, thrown on the rubbish heap when there's still lots of life in them. So I save them.

Then there's my daughter yelling at me that I have a sickness.

"What are you talking about? I always get my flu shots at the senior center. I hardly ever catch a cold."

"You're a hoarder. I saw it all on TV," she said. "We have to get you help." Clutching my hand, super dramatic. "We care for you, Mama, so we're going to make things right."

"What do I need help for? I'm doing fine. I'm happy. That's more than I can say for you." I meant it. Suzie is always complaining on the phone to me about her husband Ron's bad habits—he won't stop smoking, he leaves his underwear on the bedroom floor and his socks on the couch. As if I want to know about Ron's underwear, give me a break.

She went on and on but I tuned her out. If I hadn't learned to do that decades ago, I wouldn't be such a good-natured person, believe me.

But two weeks later Suzie showed up at the door with a woman—blond, in her forties and wearing a navy suit. This simpering bitch was a therapist and she plumped her skinny behind down on my couch, which is sideways between the walls of books and zines stacked, neatly I might say, on one wall and my entertainment section on the other wall, my 1,247 tapes. I only have about ten inches clearance between the couch and the entertainment section, but I can squeeze through, so what is the problem?

This therapist woman goes on about how hoarding is a disease but it can be treated. Then my daughter chimes in that if I don't let them come into my house and take away all my wonderful things, she will call Elder Services and have me moved into a home. For this I raised her from a squalling baby and put her through community college and paid for her wedding?

They had me over a barrel, so finally after three of these sessions with the woman who pretended to be on my side but never was, I agreed. She insisted on a tour of my house, making notes on her gizmo, talking into it. She checked the basement where I do laundry, the attic where I store stuff I don't need yet and the garage with my car in it. It turned out that same TV program that my daughter had been watching that got me into trouble was going to come to my house and film everything. They were going to clean up my house and make everything neat and orderly, the way surely I wanted it, and it wouldn't cost me a penny. They'd clear things out with my approval, of course (smirk)—with that threat hanging over my head the whole time. I was sweating by then with anxiety.

"When will all this be happening?"

She consulted her electronic gizmo. "We can schedule you for two weeks from today. The film crew will come in the day before. Then we'll have two days to clear all this junk out and clean and make your house like new again. I know it will be hard for you to adjust, but in the end, your house will be livable again."

Livable? What have I been doing here, dying? That gave me some time. I started moving my best stuff to the garage. At least I could protect that. I jammed the garage door opener so they couldn't get inside and moved my car to the driveway.

The film crew came. They moved a lot of my stuff around to make it look messy. They pushed some of the stuff from the hall into my bedroom so I could barely reach my bed that night. I could not sleep, facing the ordeal. Aside from when Walt died and when Brady had appendicitis and we just got him into the hospital in time, those two days were just about the worst of my life. They top my first delivery when I was in labor for twenty hours, the time I broke my ankle tripping on my neighbor's dog and was in a cast for a month, and the time Walt had food poisoning from some stupid mayonnaise chicken salad at a picnic. Needless to say, I didn't make that. Adele Fortunata did. Never forgave her.

They arrived early, the therapist, a cleaning crew and muscle, along with four huge semis labeled JUNK EXPRESS. Junk they called my stuff. I never picked up anything that wasn't useful. They were going to strip me bare. I had a stomachache. I couldn't eat breakfast and the coffee bored a hole in my belly.

When she saw how upset I was, the therapist took my hand as if I was a baby she was leading out of danger. "You need all these objects because you never properly processed your husband's death. It was so sudden and unexpected, you couldn't cope with the grief. You must let it out. You must experience your loss so you can let go of all these substitutes for him."

The therapist sat down with me as they carried all my precious things out to the front lawn. The neighbors were gaping. I'd never live this down. I was supposed to pick through everything and save a few things. Whatever I picked, they said I was saving too much. The therapist kept talking about processing grief. She insisted that I had never properly "processed" Walt's premature death and that hoarding, as she called it, was caused by that. Bunch of hooey. Process? Like can or freeze it? Walt didn't go collecting with me, but he liked the way I was frugal and found things instead of spending our hard-earned cash on a chair or a vase or some good reading matter. They couldn't understand how much pleasure I took in saving money and protecting good things that would otherwise end up in the dump. Finally I agreed with everything. Suzie cried and hugged me and I pretended to cry with her. I really did manage to shed a few tears when I saw them carrying out the VCRs and the Oriental rug I'd found rolled up, set out for the trash collector. I had planned to put it down in my bedroom when I had time. I'd saved four VCRs in the garage, anyhow.

"Now, what would you ever need six VCRs for? They don't even make them any longer. Don't you see how much room they take for no use?"

"How many suits do you have?"

She looked blank and stared at me. "I don't know . . . Maybe six?"

"Why not just one? And how many lipsticks?"

She ignored that. Then I saw my stuffed owl Roscoe going out into the trash. I made a grab for him.

"Now, why on earth would you want a dusty mangy old stuffed owl?"

I lied. "It belonged to my late husband."

"It's a poor substitute for him, isn't it? Can't you remember him without something probably full of dust and insect eggs?"

I loved Roscoe, his yellow eyes looking at me from the mantel. I made another grab for him but Suzie held me down in the chair. The therapist said, "If it bothers you so much, we can send it to the resale shop."

The crew along with Suzie was dividing all my property into things to be dumped and items to go to a resale shop. I found out which one. I could have tried to find out where what they were trashing was going to end up, but I am not a garbage picker and those places stink. I counted my losses but I bore with them; I had no choice. My lovely oak bookcase, my gilt elephant with a howdah on top, Walt's golf clubs, a round mirror with only a little damage to the left edge, three platters in the shape of fish, the tin of buttons, straight chairs that just needed a bit of work. I imagined running away to Florida or Mexico or Puerto Rico when they were done, to escape scrutiny, but I love my house and I know my way around here, so I sat in the lawn chair and picked through my treasures and watched them disappear. I wished for a hurricane or a blizzard, but the sky stayed blue and the day stayed mild for early November. I imagined a great wind carrying them all off and me returning to my own home, my private home, and putting everything back where I keep it. But they kept stealing my things and carting them off and I had to sit there and smile for the cameras and listen to that simpering therapist's bull dung. Inside I was boiling, but I'm not stupid, no matter what they think. They had the upper hand—for now.

Finally they had "restored" my home to what it had never looked like in all the years I'd lived there, raised my ungrateful children, been married and happy with Walt, made a life for myself that satisfied me. The therapist set up an appointment with me for some other meddler. I promised to go. I could sit through more bull dung if that would get them all off my back.

Adam and Liz had decamped before the last truck roared off with my things inside. They had a fundraiser to attend for some private school. Adam is in real estate. I don't know what he does and I don't particularly care, so long as he lets me alone. Finally Suzie, who had hung around to the bitter end—bitter for me—left, telling me how wonderful the house looked. At last they were all gone, relatives, therapist, muscle men, cleanup crew and trucks. I sat in my boring living room with only the TV for company, a single bookcase of books they'd agreed to leave me, one VCR and ten tapes. The dining room was set up for company who would never arrive. At least they cleaned everything. It does tend to get dusty, but I don't have allergies, so what do I care. I was exhausted and furious. How would you like a bunch of strangers to invade your house, take three-quarters of your possessions away, tell you what you're supposed to think and feel—all of which was being filmed for anybody in the country to gape at. I felt humiliated. I felt violated. And they had kept saying how nice it was now and expecting me to thank them. The next morning I brought my few saved treasures from the garage into the house. It still felt bare and lonely. My house and I were bereft, robbed, pillaged!

Monday I went to the bank and withdrew $500 in cash. Then I rented a U-Haul and headed for the resale shop. I figured after three days, they'd have my stuff out. I recognized twenty-three pieces of mine, so I bought them back. I told the lady I was furnishing a condo. When I unloaded the stuff into my house and set everything up, it was still barren but at least I had a few things to look at and use like that easy chair. The maroon upholstery was worn but it was comfy. Some of the glassware and dishes I'd collected, good pieces. My extra china closet that I could begin to fill. That nice table with the inlaid chessboard. A few cracks didn't spoil it. The stuffed owl, put back on the mantel. Welcome home, Roscoe. Two salad bowls. I like wood. Two end tables. I can always use end tables. Another bookcase. It was a humble beginning but better than they'd left it. I didn't feel quite so strongly I was rattling around alone in the house.

I had the locks changed so Suzie couldn't come barging in. I found some thick drapes in a different resale shop so

she couldn't see in any longer from the porch. I've learned
to protect myself. They won't catch me again. I went to the
therapist, a man this time but just as opinionated and mis-
guided as that lady. I parroted what they expected me to say.
I'm not stupid. He said he was very pleased with my progress
and my cure.

Every weekend I search for yard and garage sales and
slowly I am collecting things that make my life worthwhile,
treasures others have abandoned that I can enjoy. My home
is beginning to feel like mine again, comfy and full of
objects I have rescued. The month before last, I was on TV
and lay low for a while. The show was just as humiliating as
the experience itself. They made my home look disgusting.
I found an auburn wig in a consignment shop I put on to
go hunting now. If people stare at it, I say I had chemo and
they shut up. I know people will forget that show shortly
(there was a man on half the show who collected so many
toys and dolls he couldn't get to his bathroom; I've never
had trouble getting to mine. I love to take baths.). People
nowadays discard memories as fast as they discard perfectly
good objects. But here I am ready to save what shouldn't be
thrown on the trash heap, like this old woman and many
another. I'm gradually getting my life back, the way I like it.
I'm settling back into my home.

Going over Jordan

"Depart ye, go ye from thence, touch no unclean things; be ye clean, that bear the vessels of the Lord."

Deborah mouthed the words Brother Gentry read, her body taut to the flow from his bull throat. Then with a crackling he shut the large Bible and picked up the tract "Let Jesus In." "A wise choice of text, Brother Harman. Lead on, as the Lord chooses."

Fat-bottomed Dickie Harman, who was fifteen, just three years older than she was, took up the notes limp from his sweating hands. She wouldn't be nervous if it was her turn to lead a group, but they thought her too young. "Sister Ida, would you give us the next reading?"

Mother droned, gnawing the words. Deborah shifted on the scratchy mohair couch and a bent spring pinged. Brother Gentry wagged a thick forefinger tilted back on a chair, with his greasy briefcase gaping to spill its load of Bibles and tracts with bright violent lettering across the narrow front room.

Dickie was asking a question, and she waved her hand. "Bearing the vessels means holding to the truth, because we brethren in the truth, on the narrow way ..."

Brother Gentry boomed, "Very good, Deborah," and

she looked at Dad to see if he had noticed, but he gave her a quick frown to make her duck to her book. She wished they were doing Revelations, with its great shifting of powers and the winnowing of the chosen and the damned. She loved feeling carried on a dark wind of seeing, seeing not the worn nubs of carpet, but things that ought to be, like cedars of Lebanon, pomegranates and jacinth, and a woman upon a scarlet beast. She had been born Chosen. They said grace at every meal, and when Dad wasn't on the road selling, he would read out a chapter of the bible and pray over them. She sighed.

Through the window, a game of kick-the-can leaked in, the kids yelling and the clunk of the can off the curb. She never played. When she asked Alice if it was fun, Alice laughed at her. Mustn't think of her here. She had promised God not too. She stared at the text, trying to make it sweep her head. Her turn to read, and she must decide how to say it, the right way so the words would banner. "O God, thou my God; early will I seek thee . . ."

It was Easter vacation, but Mother kept her busy in the house all morning.

"Gone to sleep in there? I don't hear that sweeper."

"I was moving a chair." She put down "Watchfires of the Iroquois." She read all she could on Indians. Mother had spoken to her, saying they were Christians now and some even belonged to the Brethren of the Tabernacle. She'd answered, "The real ones are dead." The ones who fought, those were the real ones.

"Deborah, look at those crumbs." Mother stood with thin arms folded, her pins in the teeth expression. "You've been eating in the front room again!"

"Why clean up every speck? It only gets dirty again."

"Just because your father's away doesn't mean you can start sassing me." She drew herself up to deliver a small sermon in Dad's manner: "To be careless in any duty is to give the devil a foothold. A clean house is as important as a clean body." Her voice dropped to its ordinary singsong. "Don't I have enough worries trying to keep this house running on peanuts and never knowing when your Dad'll be home, and five calls to make for the Brethren this week? One of these fine days, it'll send me to my grave. But till then, no daughter of mine is going to be known as a sloppy individual."

No daughter of mine: as if there were ten of her. Did God care if the floor was swept? You never could tell, like that poor clod putting out his hand to keep the ark from falling, and fffft. Moving the sweeper mechanically, she reached into her mind for the scene always waiting, half played out. She had been a renegade lately. There were villains in the books, but the books were unfair. The Indians had been right, and if she had been there and not an Indian, the only thing right thing would have been to join up with them anyhow.

Finally, after three, she got away, saying she was going to the library. She ducked her head into the wind's rough grasp, liking even the grit that stung her eyes. Of course she was off to Alice's with the feeling of having paid for her afternoon. She was not allowed to play with Alice any more than the other girls were, but since she couldn't hang around with them either, she had made friends with Alice. When she was little she could not play dolls because they were graven images, and now she could not wear lipstick or go to parties. But the other girls were silly, giggling and trading stupid pictures, and Alice was brave like an Indian.

At last she came to the end of sidewalks, where the blocks of little houses like her own opened into a marshland of canals and cat o' nine tails, patched together houses and railroad tracks, bounded by the horizon of steel mills. Pillar of cloud by day and fire by night. Yanking off the scarf Mother made her wear so she wouldn't get earache

(she never got earache), she stuffed it into her pocket. The
mud felt springy though the soles of her tennis shoes and
she ran until she had put a hummock tall with the prongs
of old weeds between the neighborhood and herself, till she
was really in the Dump, as the area was called for the slag
heaps smoking far to her left. The outside place, where she
did not even feel God watching, the place where everything
came alive.

She was crossing enemy territory to send a danger mes-
sage to the tribe. She moved warily. Her head was light. Two
days before she had chewed her last pemmican. She scanned
the footsteps with the grim eye of the practiced scout. It was
many sleeps since they had passed, slim dark figures on the
ancestral trails. The mark of their burden poles was light in
the earth. They traveled quickly, alert for danger. They did
not make camp by the waterholes or the thickets where
game would lurk.

The grasses moved against the wind and she froze, fingers on the hilt of her hunting knife. A stillness, then an
orange barred cat craned out, watching with stolid amber
eyes. Hunting here, play and real: like me? She coaxed with
her lips and the cat leaned: then turned with a deep meow
and tail-up slipped into deeper weeds.

Coming out on the tracks, she balanced along a shiny
rail for a hundred feet. A row of empty boxcars squatted
weatherworn on the far tracks. Scuffling from one. A cracked
adolescent voice called, "Hey kid, looking for action? Hey,
c'mere." Somebody inside laughed in a squeal. Her foot
slipped, twisted.

"Hey kid, you wanna see something?"

Stubbornly she kept her pace, jumping on every third
tie. A train made the rails hum, so when she was well past
the boxcar, she crouched in the cinders of the embankment,
waiting. A diesel pulling a long freight. As it rushed toward
her, she caught her breath and could not let it out until the

engine had ripped past. She felt torn as it rolled away, leaving her in the cinders. Names on the cars rode above. Where it would go, cities shone like scrubbed metal; when it came from prairies spread wide and towns with names like Crazy Horse were flung against the tracks and sullen under too much sky, mountains rose into wilderness and eagles and glaciers.

She followed the sluggish brown canal to Alice's in a straggle of two-families with faces to a road and backs to the canal and rickety docks. An old Dodge stood on blocks in the yard, and Jackie and another kid were kneeling on the springs. As she passed by they sprayed her with noise: "eheheheheheh, you're dead!"

She went up the outside stairs, pushing a pop bottle and broken bamboo rod out of her way, rapped, then stood back and yelled, "Alice!"

Livy, the nine-year-old, let her in. "Allie! Deborah's here!"

Alice came languidly from the kitchen, twisting a rubber band between her fingers and letting it snap into her palm. "Boy, am I sick and tired trying to clean this mess," she said like a mother. "Ma's coming back early today. Or so she says." Dropping on a cot, she grabbed Livy. "Let me do your hair."

"Don't stick your dirty nails in me!"

Alice took Livy's stringy yellow hair and plaited it deftly, looping the rubber band around the end. "So look who's here. Big deal. Where you been all week?"

"We had company one night, and Mother had me cleaning. She wouldn't let me out."

Alice smiled her closed little smile. She was only a year and a half older, but she'd been menstruating two years already and her body was rounding. She had whitish hair, silky and sparse, which she teased out like a winter bush. Her eyes were long and silver-grey. She had almost no brows. "Go play with Jackie," she told Livy.

"Go screw yourself." Livy threw herself on a chair, letting her feet swing as she waited in bored expectation.

"Want to go out, Alice? Let's take the rowboat."

"It's too cold." Alice picked at the loose polish on her thumb. "Besides, I got to clean. Didn't you hear?" She sauntered into the kitchen, Deborah behind her, and began running water for the pile of dishes. Wary and disappointed, Deborah took a towel to dry. Out in the boat in the maze of canals, they were a gang hiding out, explorers in the Amazon. Alice stepped into her games with a matter of fact readiness, for behind her mask she dreamed too. Best, Alice was a serious Indian or explorer: she asked what they would eat, she insisted they have shelter and histories. If she were a man that day, she peed with her legs apart standing because she said that was how men did. And the game was real and it worked.

The door slammed behind Livy. Alice smiled with her wan mouth. "Saw Crow yesterday."

"You didn't talk to him." She heard her voice pleading.

"It's a free country. He was standing on the corner by Jaegar's. He whistles, but I just look right through him, just like I never seen him. He yells, 'Hey Blondie,' but I keep on walking. So he starts cussing me, so I turn around and give it back good. He tried to make a date for Saturday, but I told him where to go."

"Why did you talk to him?"

They finished the dishes in silence. Crow was skinny and mean and leathery, the first in their class to carry better than a jackknife. Deborah hated Crow because Alice had gone in the weeds with him. Alice said he was the only one, but that was a fib. She would never say anything, or Alice would keep at her till she pretended to believe, but she longed for Alice to be grandly bad, flamboyantly bad, in big proud gaudy awning stripes of evil.

"Guess what, Georgia's knocked up again." Georgia was Alice's older sister who lived downstairs.

"Again? They're crowded already."

"That pig Ralph. He won't use nothing."

"Use something?"

"Cheez, don't you know anything?"

"Use something? You mean like you told me Nancy did?"

"No. There's things you use. Know what Trojans are?"

Helen of Troy and the pagans: but that wasn't what Alice was on. "No."

"Look, come in Ma's room and I'll show you what she uses."

Alice felt around in a bureau drawer until she pulled out a hot water bottle with a long cord. Deborah frowned. "Hey, I've seen them. My mother has one. She said it was for enemas."

Alice laughed. "The lines she hands you sometimes!"

Her mother in the nether world of the Dump. Sister Gentry had no children. Was that why?

Alice stood at her mother's dresser applying a thick coat of makeup. "Want to show you something. I tried this yesterday, and wait'll you see." She dabbed mascara awkwardly on her few lashes. "I've been practicing." Giving her hair a fluff, she turned for admiration.

"You look fifteen or sixteen, honest!"

"Pretty good, huh?" Alice made eyes at the mirror, rolling her thin hips and tossing her hair. "I'm getting rigged up like this some night when Ma's not home," she said grandly. "You bet the boys will pay attention."

Deborah sat at the mirror, picking up a lipstick. She pressed too hard and a hunk broke off. Her face looked young and crowded next to Alice.

"My mouth's too big."

"Don't let it get you down," Alice shrugged. "They're supposed to be good for kissing." They scrubbed their faces at the washbowl. The towels always felt like frog skin.

Alice peeled potatoes at the wobbly table. "That shitheel

Ralph makes me see red. I'm never getting married. I won't end up with a man kicking me around and telling me what to do. Do that! Stay outa there! None of that for me." Alice's favorite topic.

"Listen, how soon is your Ma really coming home?"

"Two hours, maybe. Three?" She chopped the potatoes and dropped them into a pot of water on the sink.

It was no good, making all those promises, ever since that Saturday she had secretly gone to a movie with Alice. Afterwards, they had been acting it with Alice as the outlaw and her as the girl he held prisoner. In the movie, he kissed her, but Alice said she would show her what really happened, and she put her hand under Deborah's skirt. Since then, they played the captured girl with pirates and spies, but touching was always part of the game. God and her mother would damn her anyway for coming to see Alice, so she might as well be damned all the way. "Let's go in your Ma's room and play prisoners."

Alice smiled tightly. "Don't want to."

"Why not?"

"I want to go down to Brand Street. I want a coke."

"We could go later."

"No, I want to go now." Alice reached up in the cupboard and took change from a cup. She looked over her shoulder as she put on the coat that had been her Ma's. "Sometimes I'm sorry I showed you. You're as bad as a guy."

"You taught me because you wanted to! You do this to keep me in line." She pulled on her jacket, shoving her fists into the pockets where her scarf was knotted. "Needn't be so sure I'll go with you."

"Don't bother. I got friends. Maybe I'll see Crow."

"Shut up. I'll go. But I'm broke."

"I'll treat you."

She was angry all the way and would not talk, but she knew that was useless: Alice could sit with that little smile for days. She never spoke in school. If the teacher called on her, she would only say "I don't know" in a flat voice. Usually Alice didn't know, but Deborah heard her say it even when she did. They sat diagonally in homeroom, in opposite corners, because the pupils were seated by grades and behavior. She felt rotten when the teacher would start needling Alice, trying to show how stupid she was. She would feel guilty, especially if she were called on right after and she would have the answer. She wanted to say that she too did not know, but she couldn't. And to anybody, she was a good girl and Alice was bad. That ate at her, and she thought sometimes that she should stand up and explain, but who would listen?

"Alice, I'm sorry I was snotty. But you shouldn't push me. You do it too often."

"Let's go in the dime store."

Her stomach squeezed itself. The test again. She followed Alice between the garish counters under the hillbilly screech of the loudspeaker, a brave facing his initiation. But an Indian proved his right to his adult name once, while she was tested and tested by Alice. If she lost her nerve, Alice would turn away, lumping her with the girls who giggled, who traded singers' pictures, who gave parties to which neither were invited.

At the jewelry counter, Alice palmed a charm bracelet. Deborah's job was to watch the salesgirls and shield Alice. At the candy counter, Alice bought a quarter bag of nonpareils, and took a fire-engine whistle off the toy counter to join it. "For Jackie."

She left Alice abruptly. Today she must press her nerve, test herself harder than Alice tested her. She stopped by cosmetics. "Can I help you?" The saleslady was fat. As she leaned on the register to ease her feet, her large breasts flowed forward like melted butter.

"Do you have any polish remover?"

"Over here," As the girl turned, Deborah shot out her

hand and grabbed a bottle of nail polish. She stuffed her clenched fist into her pocket, hiding it under the scarf. "That's not big enough." She felt sweated. She had not even looked to see if anybody was watching. The manager might be right behind her.

"What's wrong with it, kid? That's all we got."

They'd call the police, they'd call her mother. Her skin prickled and burned like poison ivy. "She said a big bottle," mumbling, "thank you." In agony, she turned. Backs of women. No one, the aisle swam. She hurried to find Alice, staring at the goldfish and eating candy.

As they walked out, she said, "You want this?"

Alice took the bottle, holding its nail against her own. "Sure, Siren Pink. It's a good one." She laughed, suddenly, with her whole body, squeezing the bottle before she tucked it away. "I'll try it as soon as we get back. Presents you're given are better than the ones you take."

Side by side on stools, they sipped chocolate cokes and talked about money. "I'll have a ranch in California, right on the Pacific with the waves rolling up. Eight cats and eight collies—I'll raise them together. A plane I can fly. And a boat to sail all over the world."

"I want a mink and so much money I can walk in them stores downtown and say charge it, and nobody'll blink."

"You could come too. We'll sail around from island to island, eating coconuts, and we'll find an orphan chimpanzee and make him a pet. We can go swimming off the side ... "

Alice's straw rasped on the bottom of her glass. "We'll have a high old time, nobody to boss us around."

She shielded Alice on the way out, to lift a bag of potato chips. Alice tore an end off and they passed it. She whistled in snatches, thinking how she'd got the polish, and how Alice had laughed with pleasure, her face bright. Then her stomach sank and bits of chip lay on her tongue like wooden splinters. If they were caught, and they would be!

"Maybe Ma won't be home yet." Alice looked sideways, smiling. "I bet she won't."

That night at the Tabernacle, Deborah waited as her mother chatted in the anteroom. "I said to him, John, if you buy that TV set, you let a new snare of Satan's into our very midst."

"No man can serve two masters—"

"I said to him, if you're sitting watching scantily-clad women and people shooting each other, you aren't thinking about God. And think of children seeing beer commercials day in and day out."

She tapped Mother's arm. "Mama, I'm going in."

"Save us good seats, Deborah. Near the front."

She walked into the cross-shaped room filled with folding chairs. A picture of Christ the Shepherd stood at the far end, surrounded by banked gladiolas. The speaker's lectern was centered in the little stage before it, "I shall not die, but live and declare the words of the LORD," on a banner above. "Advertise the LORD!"

After the opening prayer, Brother Gentry lit into the night's topic, the Last Judgment. "When ye therefore shall see the abomination of desolation and expect those days should be shortened, there should be no flesh saved: but for the elect's sake, those days shall be shortened . . ."

She felt suddenly, this is not me. On the folding chairs, all about her were the Elect, the lambs of God: but she stole and lied and played dirty games and the Dump she loved better than the Tabernacle.

"And He shall send his angels with a great sound of a trumpet . . . There shall two be in the fields: the one shall be taken and the other left . . . And these shall go away into everlasting punishment, but the righteous into life eternal."

She grieved for herself, standing among the damned in a dusky field, their faces upturned to the dissolving skies where angels darted like comets carrying off the virtuous.

She was wrong with Alice, yes, and Alice would end it by pushing too hard. But her affections were back in the wrong corner now, instead of with the faithful at the head of the cosmos. She did not love the Elect: they were clean and law-abiding, they washed in the sight of God and ate their peas and answered the right words, they sat on straight chairs without daydreaming. They marched, they did not play games that came alive, or test each other, and never would she make one of them laugh as Alice had when she had given her the stupid stolen polish. What they had, they kept.

One winter evening when she was ten, she had been let out to play and built an altar of snow. In the alley she found a vase glazed with flowers. She set it on the altar as an offering. The next morning, wanting to take the vase in, she hit it on the sidewalk to knock the snow out. It broke in her hands. She had realized then she couldn't cheat God.

Time for the closing prayer. She bowed her head but did not follow obediently the words of Brother Gentry. No, not for her. She walked, tall and alone, beneath a sky of thunder clouds toward black mountains ragged with flames. She had made a pact with the grim, all-seeing God, and He had closed his books on her. Her ribs burned with joy and fright: she was free, she was outside, she walked into the wind.

They were driving back when Mother remarked in an overly casual tone, "By the way, Brother Gentry said you could conduct the next study meeting. Isn't that something for a girl your age."

God had not told Brother Gentry about her yet. Or was He bargaining? Too late. "I can't do it."

"Don't be scared. God will give you the right words. We'll study it over beforehand."

Mother wanted her to. For once they would be pleased. She wanted to say, Mama, I'd do it for you if I still could. "I can't go to the meeting."

"Can't?" Mother scowled. "What kind of nonsense is that?"

The neon lit storefronts of Brand Street. Mother never did understand about Indians, and she would never see why you had to be a renegade, how you got damned and joined the other side. Loneliness was cold and wind-struck. She had to make Mother let go, or they would coax and batter her till she was halfway Chosen again. "I don't believe in God anymore."

"What?" Mother slammed on the brakes, throwing them forward.

"I've lost my faith," she mumbled. "I won't be going with the Brethren after this." Her voice sound so stiff and funny, she felt a nervous smile tweak at her lips.

Mother started the car again, turning sharp into their street. "I don't know who's been at you. Wait till your father hears! I'm going up to that school and see who's been poisoning your mind! You hear me?"

"I decided all by myself."

"What have you been reading behind my back? Wait till your father gets home, just wait! You're going, all right."

"No." A game of kick-the-can broke, scattering kids to let the car pass. The sky full of stars above the huddle of wooden houses was the universe of God's faithful, but she would be strong as a tree in the wind, and be damned with a little smile like Alice's.

Her stomach wriggled cold and slippery. Mother would go to school. Mother would shout about religion and everyone would make fun of Deborah. The teachers would laugh behind their hands in the hall. She could still take it back. But no, she could not promise and promise anymore. She would laugh, instead, far out ahead of Alice and her coughing and mother and Crow and Georgia, she would test herself and be loyal to her test like an Indian at the Sun dance, till her renegade's laughter puzzled the obedient stars.

Scars

In 1968 I spent the summer in Cuba. I was one of the founders of the North American Congress on Latin America, one of the few New Left organizations that still flourishes, putting out an excellent magazine covering issues, events and conflicts south of the border you would never read about elsewhere. It was because of that connection I was invited to come.

The CIA terrorized us on the way from Mexico to Cuba. But the story I want to tell you is about a trip I took with friends who had come down later and with our guide Lohania to Santiago de Cuba. It is one of the parts of Cuba—near the Sierra Maestra—that has the strongest African traditions still current. It's an old city of mostly white or cream colored buildings and from the hotel we looked down on tile roofs the color of orange sherbet and rusty metal ones, the steep descent to the bay below. Most of the streets climbed up or skidded down. Many of the buildings dated to the colonial period. The huge mountains of the Sierra Maestra crowded in on the city as it crouched around the stunning bay with its busy port and its glittering beaches. Lohania had arranged for us to be there during Summer Carnival when the Revolution is celebrated. The streets were crowded day and night. We heard drums, we heard small orchestras, we heard singing and from little kids on up to great grandmas, people danced in the bars, on the beach, in the street. It all led up to the 26th of July when it felt like half the population was marching, dancing in the streets. Lohania had arranged for us to watch from the balcony of one of those beige Spanish buildings that held offices, but we insisted on being down in the street.

The *candombes* marched, each with their *santos* and their drum rhythms. Each *candombe* used different rhythms, passed down from generation to generation. The dancers were like congeries of parrots and parakeets, dressed up like *Santería* gods and goddesses, like pirates, like guerrilla fighters, like caricatures of colonial aristocrats. *Santería* had been forbidden under Batista but was alive and vibrant after the revolution. Group after group passed us where we stood, in eye-scorching colors like huge tropical birds, weaving and dancing, beating on big and little drums, skin and tin. We danced along with the drums and shared local beer and occasional Cuba Libres with the locals and street food—Cuban sandwiches, the toasted peanuts in paper cones called *maníes*, *plátano* chips, *papas rellenas*. We drank a lot of *guarapo*, freshly ground sugar cane juice. And we danced.

We were staying in an old faded stucco hotel on a hill with a swimming pool and it was hot. It was humid. The air felt like a wet wool blanket except at the beach. Even at night the temperature dropped at most ten degrees. We had noticed that Lohania always wore pants even on the most sultry days. While we frolicked in the pool to cool off, she sat fully dressed on the side. When we went to the beach, she sat clothed and read among the females of all ages in bikinis. We wondered among ourselves if this was some kind of excess modesty, unusual in the Cuban culture. We were used to seeing woman carrying machine guns with their hair in curlers, party dresses under their camouflage, women wearing sexy tops or tight, short dresses at the common street dances or dances in private homes or institutions to which we were invited. Cuba was a sensual place. Women dressed up or down as they chose. But it was hot. Why the constant cover-up? We wondered privately whether the Party was trying to institute some new standards of dress or behavior.

Lohania was of medium height, slender, with erect posture I envied and skin deeply tanned with hair the color of a good brown sauce. She wore a long braid often draped over her shoulder. Her eyes were dark and large. She was strong physically and usually quite verbal. Her English was workmanlike, but she came alive in Spanish. She could only joke in her native language. She could dance well and when we had to climb the steep hills, we got out of breath long before she did. She would grab our luggage and haul it up the stairs before we could stop her.

On the 27th, the carnival was winding down. My friends went off to visit the huge old fort that loomed over the bay, San Pedro de Roca, but I thought it too hot to stumble around the stones in mid-afternoon. A local guide had been provided, so Lohania stayed with me.

Finally I asked her about her modesty, not sure if it was polite, but consumed with curiosity. We had become friendly on our excursions. I'd been in Cuba longer than the others and at that time, my Spanish was excellent. I'd studied it in high school and for two years in college, but that wasn't the reason I was fluent. Living on the Upper West Side of Manhattan, I used it daily with the local bodega, my drycleaner, the greengrocer, the guys in the building who were all from the Dominican Republic.

We were crossing the patio where the pool was crowded with adults swimming and children splashing. "Why don't you ever swim? Don't you know how? I don't swim well myself, but I like to get wet and cool down."

She was silent for a couple of minutes. "I swim when

I'm alone on a stretch of beach. That's easy here. We have so many beaches."

I waited. She sighed and then she pulled up her left pant leg. On the flesh of her calf were large wounds that had healed but had left gruesome-looking, puckered and discolored scars. They were a couple of inches across, circular, raised. They were scattered along her leg as far as she let me see.

"Were you attacked by a dog? A large animal? Or is that from the fighting?" I knew she would have been quite young then, but our driver had joined his mother in the mountains when he was fifteen.

She motioned for me to sit down on the low wall that surrounded the pool and began her story. Behind us, the palms rustled in the salty breeze and a gecko peered at us from the shingled-looking bark. She tossed her braid over her shoulder and frowned, rolling her pant leg back down. She was silent for a few minutes and I waited, watching the gecko scamper up the palm bark. She spoke slowly. She had been part of the brigades of young people sent out into the countryside all over Cuba in the literacy campaign—the analphabetization. Most Cubans who were not middle class, especially in the country, had no education and could not read a word. She had been sent to what had been before the revolution the King Ranch, a huge area where the American corporation raised cattle and feed.

"It was hard to teach there. Most of the children suffered from kwashiorkor. They wanted badly to learn, but words slipped through their minds. Concentration was so difficult for them."

I didn't know what the word *kwashiorkor* meant. Lohania explained that it is a deficiency disease caused by not having enough protein in the diet. It is especially hard on infants, toddlers, children.

"On a cattle ranch?"

But the workers and their children did not get beef. Kwashiorkor causes brain damage and makes learning far more difficult.

"Is that what you had?"

She laughed. "You can't catch it. It's a deficiency disease only. No, I went barefoot part of the time because I felt funny wearing shoes when none of the kids had them. There are worms in the soil that eat their way into your feet. They live in your body doing damage for months but when they are ready, they chew their way out. It leaves these ugly scars."

"I'm so sorry. That you should be left scarred from trying to help people."

"Everyone there had them. The worms were endemic. So while I was there, I didn't mind the sores so much."

"But now you do. You must regret that happened to you."

"Mostly it was a good experience for me. I never knew how badly so many of my people lived. The scars remind me of what we were fighting to change." She pulled her pant leg back down. "But they do embarrass me. I think if I were a better Communist, they wouldn't." She grimaced. "But I don't like people to look at me with pity. I don't like people to think I'm deformed. So I hide my scars."

I thought to myself that maybe we all have scars we hide. I didn't go around telling people how I had almost died from a self-induced abortion that had left me anemic, bone-thin and weak. And scared. I was as obsessive about birth control as she was about covering up her legs. My mother had concealed her age till her death, never admitting she was ten years older than my father. I knew, but he didn't, that she had been married twice before him, not once.

"Can I tell my companions your story?"

"Just keep it to yourself. I don't like to be pitied."

"I don't pity you. I admire you." I lied. Both were true.

She's Dying, He Said

Circa 1943

I was what was then called a tomboy until halfway through
my seventh year. I had always played with neighboring boys.
I had little interest in school—being just average and paying
little attention. Then I caught the German measles followed
quickly by rheumatic fever. The doctor came, examined me,
said I would die and asked for his ten dollars in cash.

My grandmother Hannah who lived with us half the
year and half with my mother's youngest sister Ruth came
on the train from Cleveland. I have vague feverish memories.
I felt like my mother and father were angry with me for
being so sick. My *bobbelah* rushed into action. My Hebrew
name was Miriam. The first thing Hannah did was conduct
an impromptu naming ceremony as if I were a newborn.
There was a guy present I remember dressed all in black
with *peyeses* and speaking Hebrew, so it might have been
a rabbi she pressed into service. She changed my name to
Marah, bitter, so that *moloch ha moves*, the angel of death,
would not know me, and would not want me and would
pass over.

She hung on my neck a *hamsa*, that upraised hand with
the eye in the palm, to ward off the demons that were attack-
ing me. I have it to this day, although the string on which

she hung it has long ago fallen apart. She said it protected me against *ayin harah*, the evil eye, from which diseases and curses come.

Most of this occurred when my father was absent. He was not Jewish and resented any religious observation. He would go to the Presbyterian Church when we were visiting his relatives in Ebensburg, Pennsylvania, in soft coal country, but he did not believe in a deity. He was stolidly materialist rooted in what science he knew and understood, believing passionately in mathematics and rationality—except when he lost his massive and fiery temper. He regarded any Jewish usage as superstitious, unclean, messy. My grandmother who had given me my religious education was Orthodox. When she was with us, we ate kosher. My mother managed to make it acceptable to him without telling him much of what was going on. He would insist on dairy with his meat, but the rest of us avoided it quietly. I grew up understanding that being Jewish was a secretive thing in Detroit, but not in Cleveland. When Hannah went back to Ruth, our level of observance dropped to zero. No more Shabbat candles, no prayers, no singing except of popular songs.

I was racked by fever, slipping in and out of consciousness. I remember waking and smelling something burning. I still don't know what herbs my *bobbelah* set on fire in an ashtray, but again, she was driving out the demons. She surrounded my bed with a rim of kosher salt. My mother, being a superstitious woman herself, let Hannah do what she could but hung back, mostly I think from fear of what my father would say if he found out. He did not come into my sickroom—it had been my brother's bedroom but he had gone off to the Marines to fight in the Pacific. Until he left home, I slept in my parents' room.

The herbs were burned while my father was at work, fixing machinery for Westinghouse that frequently took him all over Michigan. He was gone for days at a time all through my childhood, and with me sick and presumably dying, he was gone as much as possible. That made Hannah's activities much easier to carry out. He never smelled the herbs, he never saw the salt, he didn't notice the hand hung on a string around my neck. The rabbi came and went without his knowledge. Saving me was a secret between my grandmother and my mother. But Hannah was the one who did all the work.

I began to be conscious more and more. Whenever I woke, Hannah was praying over me in Yiddish. Although she was the daughter of a rabbi back in Lithuania near the border with Russia, part of the Pale of Settlement to which Jews were confined (except for prostitutes much in demand and boys taken for the Tsar's army who seldom survived to return), Hannah did not know Hebrew. She knew Yiddish, of course, Russian, Lithuanian, some German and heavily accented English, but she regarded herself as almost illiterate because she was ignorant of Hebrew. Women often prayed in their own language while the men prayed in Hebrew. She often spoke to me in Yiddish but I answered in English. I have no idea why this was how it was. Somehow it was expected.

I can close my eyes and see her rocking back and forth davening in a singsong, almost musical voice, standing over my bed. She was a small woman in height, like my mother, like me—particularly as I age and shrink. Unlike other Orthodox women, she had long hair and not a wig because my grandfather, dead ten years by this time, had forbidden her to cut it. He said if any angels were tempted, they would have to come through him to get at her. Sometimes when I opened my eyes, I would see her with her hair braided round her head, occasionally covered with a kerchief. Sometimes when I woke, I would see her as she came to bed with me, her long chestnut hair streaked with white tumbling down, cascading around her shoulders. In her seventies, she had lush hair like a waterfall and it smelled good, not perfume, something else. Once she had been entirely beautiful, but giving birth to eleven children in poverty and sometimes in danger had robbed her. Her face was puffy and wrinkled, her eyes glazed with cataracts that would eventually blind her from doing embroidery for money. She was stooped and round. But her face when she prayed almost glowed in the twilight of my room where the blinds were closed and the curtains drawn. She was talking to G-d, imploring him, demanding, begging, speaking to him as a wife might speak to a husband in those days. Reminding him of the good things, the *mitzvot*, she had done, giving *tzedakah* to the poor even when she too was poor, taking in an orphan when she already had so many children, lest the child be neglected. Now it was Ha Shem's turn to do right by her granddaughter.

I began to be aware of the voices from the house next door, right across their driveway from us. I heard kids playing in the street, allye, allye-outsinfree. I heard the ice cream truck jingling its tune, the horse clopping past pulling the car of the fruit and vegetable man, the knife sharpener calling to housewives. I had been gone from the world into a hot dark place of nightmares, gone from life. Now I was slowly coming back to my bed, my sickroom, my Hannah, my tuxedo cat Buttons who was now allowed to visit me.

I remember the first day I could sit up in bed. My mother read me a story from a book I loved, about an adventurous goat. I remember eating raspberry-flavored rennet pudding. I remember my mother's chicken soup, of which I could take a little. Usually I helped her make it. We would pluck the feathers together and burn off any remaining nubs. Sometimes we made dusters of the feathers, tying them together. My mother added the unborn eggs to the soup.

Everything felt new and precious, but when I tried to stand, I fell. I had lost half my body weight. Photos from before show a slightly chubby kid with banged up knees and a big grin always doing something. Nobody in my family took any more photos of me till I was in high school, when girlfriends took them of each other. When I returned to school in the fall, I was pale blue, you could barely see me if I stood sideways, and I fainted a lot. I was as weak as a kid could be and survive. From a strong active tomboy, I turned into a bullied nerd who began to read a lot and excel in school. It was all I was good at now. I believed my *bobbelah* had saved me, but for what I wasn't sure. My old pleasures were gone. My parents seemed to be ashamed of me, especially after I was diagnosed as nearsighted by the school nurse and sent with my mother to have my eyes tested and fitted with a cheap pair of glasses. Four eyes, I was now. I was regularly beaten up, especially by the Polish Catholic kids. Only my old alliance with the African American girls saved me sometimes. I escaped into books. I wrote stories about my heroic cat Buttons. The books I liked the best were animal stories because it didn't matter if it was Lad or Lassie who was saving the drowning boy. Girl animals could have real adventures and be heroes. The other kind of books I liked were adventure stories supposed to be for boys. The girls teased me about the books I read during library periods. I didn't care. The books for girls were insipid. The weaker I was, the more I dreamed of having superpowers, of great deeds, of harrowing adventures on the high seas or in space or in the jungle. I still loved going to Cleveland, when I could go to *shul* with Hannah and the other ladies would make a fuss over me. I liked being with women only. It felt safe and warm.

By the time I was twelve, I had regained my strength although not my good eyesight. That I would never get back. But I could walk ten miles, I could run faster than all but one Black long-legged girl in my school, I began to hold my own in fights. I had friends again.

When as an adult I was studying with Reb Zalman, he admired my golem novel *He, She and It*. One day he asked me my Hebrew name. I told him. He was displeased. He changed it to Ma'ora, bringer of light. I said I would hyphenate but I could not abandon the name my Hannah had given me when everyone said I was dying and had given up on me—except her. I honor her with the Hebrew name of bitterness that she gave me so the angel of death would pass on—and it did. And I lived and grew up to write about her and many others whose stories would otherwise be lost.

Somebody Who Understands You

We were all in love with Mr. Danelli, every one of us girls on the high school newspaper, the *Signpost*, and more besides who'd had him for English and still dropped in to talk. His first name, we knew from Laura who was a study hall aide and peeked in his file, was Domenico, but the other faculty called him Dan. He was short, stocky, intense with dark brown hair combed over the reddening center of his scalp. His eyebrows were coarse and jaunty over his big grin. He would look you directly in the eyes, leaning forward, till you were sure no one could interest him more. Besides, he had the habit when talking of touching your hand or forearm or if you were standing, your shoulder. His hands were always warm.

I used to wonder why he endured us: lonely, over-imaginative girl nerds bringing him our writing, our drawings, our videos or merely our troubles to his corner desk in the *Signpost* office. "My mother won't let me ..." "My father took away my cellphone for a month just because ..." "I need a car, really I do, and will they listen?" "Everybody lies all the time!" "School is a waste of time." "Do you think I'm queer?" "Why does everybody bully me?" "I hate my brother!" "Do you believe in telepathy?" "... and he never called me back!" In the world we were rebelling against, jammed in aging tract houses between the half-empty mall and the abandoned car parts factory, he stood torch high, our embodiment of the intelligent liberal.

When any new girl came into the *Signpost* office, he would call them over for an interview. He could spot the type of gauche eager nerd that interested him in five minutes. Don't imagine he was scouting for sex; physical contact never went further than that touch on the hand or shoulder.

He had friends among the younger faculty, married men and unmarried women who sent students in to be mined. He liked to think of himself as better at departmental politics than he was; we knew that the principal, the chairman of the English Department and the other brass didn't quite trust him. He was much too friendly with students. We felt protective. Almost we wished him to be in danger of being fired, so we could rush to his defense. But being one of the only faculty who taught a couple of courses at the community college gave him some kind of prestige. He was one of the few teachers with a PhD.

During our second intimate talk, he invited me to use him as a father confessor—his idea of his relationship with us. Well, we confessed everything but our collective passion. A few into drugs or drink dared tell him. Muffled rivalries clashed about him. Heather or Kelly would walk in while I was pouring out my father's callousness and would search for something in the filing cabinet behind him until she got rid of me.

He did more than sympathize: he polished us—oh, roughly, but we were as spiny as sea urchins. He taught me to say Moht-zart, what I should admit liking to read, the location of the only good bookstore in our city, not to dress as if my body were two sizes larger. He determined our beliefs as thoroughly as any church: a highly partisan Democratic interest in politics and civil liberties, a craftsman pose that people were to be admired who did anything well, no matter if it were cake- or poem-making, pitching or playing the violin, playing tennis or singing the blues.

Yet what did we love but the steadiness of his dark gaze that seemed to see us whole as we wanted to be seen and the warmth of his hands, his vulgar humor. His was the only real animal presence among the faculty. No one but me ever saw the poems Kelly wrote about him. I remember she used sun imagery.

Kelly Aimes was his favorite that year, as she had been the year before. She was a year ahead of me, brilliant, becoming attractive in a rose and auburn way. I envied her. Yet she was desperately lonely. Her parents were divorced, her mother bitter and mistrustful and madly possessive. More than a helicopter parent, she wrapped herself around her daughter like a net. If Kelly told her mother she was stopping after school at my house, Mrs. Aimes would call her to check. Mrs. Aimes would harass her with questions if an errand took longer than expected. Her senior year, her mother put a GPS on her cell that showed where Kelly was at all times. Yet she did not complain as I did. I would hear Mr. Danelli's deep voice, intimate and mocking by turns, and her quick passionate soprano. A pal of his who taught algebra would drop by between classes. Mr. Danelli would lean back in his chair grinning in easy camaraderie while Kelly sat tense and impatient, ignoring the intruder.

"How goes it, Dan?"

"Performing the seven life functions. How was the meeting?"

"Another cop in the school. The scandal of a few butts in the urinals. How's Pat?"

Pat was the wife. A couple of times when he had me over on a Sunday, I met her. Kelly went oftener. Somehow Mr. Danelli had charmed Mrs. Aimes into believing he was a good influence on her daughter, so Kelly could visit without an armed escort.

Pat was plump and full-bodied, with straw-blond hair and wide brown eyes. We had grudgingly to admit that for a woman her age, she was not bad although she should lose twenty pounds. Brandon was ten, Ethan, five, and Emily, two. They were harder to swallow than Pat: the tricycle on the lawn, the litter of toys, the bathtub rimmed with rubber ducks, a potty you had to pick off the toilet. I was a little shocked that the kids spent much of Sunday watching TV in what he called The Animal Room.

The house itself surprised me. It was way out in a suburb I'd never heard of where streets were called lanes and named for revolutionary war battles. Although the houses were newish, the trees had not all been chopped down. There was a wall of windows giving on to the rather straggly garden with a basketball hoop and a gas grill. The whole first floor was one huge room except for the kitchen, which seemed weird to me because the stove was in a granite island in the middle of the floor. The chairs were high stools like I'd seen when I passed the dim bar The Cozy Corner although it wasn't on a corner and reeked of beer and stale smoke on my way from the bus to our house. This ceiling was high but sloped and a tiled fireplace stuck up all the way. He told me his father had built it for them and I was naïve enough to think he meant by hand.

Supper included the first artichokes I had ever tried to eat, then shrimp and spaghetti, which they called pasta. I helped scrape dishes for the dishwasher. Then we sat before the fireplace while jazz played. His wife served sherry that he let me taste but not drink, then occupied herself putting the children to bed before it was time for him to drive me all the way back home. Kelly said Pat was omnipresent but seldom in the room. I didn't like her either. Kelly said they had married while he was still in graduate school. We fancied that they had to get married. She said his father was a wealthy contractor Dan detested. The father had tried to force Dan into his business, where Pat's two brothers functioned and grew fat and powerful.

We knew he was bored with high school. He taught a couple of night courses at the community college. "Why don't you teach full-time there? Or at the city college?" I asked him. We felt he was too good to be wasted here—once we were gone, of course.

"You know how many applicants there are for every position? Grad schools turn out ten PhDs for every available job. I get paid almost nothing for those courses—not enough to keep one of my kids in clothes for half a year. We're too used to living beyond our means, anyhow."

You have to put writing first, he'd tell us, or music or art or dancing. Art was a discipline of mind and body. If one of us produced an artifact that pleased him, he'd flood her with praise and confidence. I remember prancing home filled with a sense of expectation so intense I felt the streets should ring with music.

Other times he would be abrupt, leering. Once Kelly and I came in to ask him about colleges. He listened wearily. Then he looked at us with intense disgust. "What does it matter where you go? You'll get married, put your husband through and then the five D's will take over."

I let Kelly ask him what they were. "Dishes, daddy, diapers, discontent and then, finally, divorce."

"Think that's clever? Better than eraser dust, Eliot and exhibitionism. Up your ego!" She walked out.

Every other week they spatted. Only two days after that I overheard him telling her, "Never mind these idiots. Someday you'll meet a man who can appreciate you, your mind as well as your looks."

I remembered that conversation the next spring when Kelly came back to see us during spring break from the state college. "You're looking fit," he told her. "I like your hair long."

She was boiling with news. She loved college. Her

English professor thought her poetry showed talent. The dormitory was so noisy she bought herself earplugs. She sat on the edge of his desk, swinging her ankle. Her old tense defensive posture was gone. "I met this music student. He's twenty. We're sharing a dorm room but I think we'll move out to an apartment next fall ..."

He waved me out of the room. The rest of the conversation I heard from Kelly, sputtering over coffee. "He implied I was being an idiot. That I'd fallen for the first guy who ever paid me any attention. That all Mason wants is sex—somebody he's never met. That I'd get pregnant and have to drop out of college. That I was throwing my life away ... and on and on. He sounded like my mother."

"Does she know?"

"Are you kidding? The two times she drove up to visit me, we moved his stuff out and my girlfriend Chloe pretended to be my roommate. Mason and I, we're both thinking of going to summer school so we can stay together."

"Will your mother let you?" After all, she was paying most of the bills the scholarship didn't cover.

"I'll sell it to her as a way to graduate faster and save money. She's afraid of taking out a loan. She has a terror of owing money, from when my father dumped her and left her with a mortgage." She shook her head. "I just can't believe how absolutely uncool Mr. Danelli turned out to be. He kept berating me like I'd done something terribly wrong. I mean, I was a virgin till Mason. Half our class were fucking their boyfriends by junior year—or sucking them off, anyhow. It isn't like I'm screwing the football team! He's a major disappointment. Don't trust him with your secrets anymore, believe me."

I wondered if he were jealous. After all, Kelly had been his favorite. I was just one of his chaste harem of nerdy girls. I even wondered if perhaps he knew something about Mason that Kelly didn't. After she returned to college, he lectured all of us about what a mistake Kelly had made, "None of you will ever do anything but breed like your mothers. Is that what you want, to end up in a decaying tract house in a decaying neighborhood in a dying city?" I said I didn't think she'd done anything tragic, or even unusual. He roared and lectured for two weeks and then he stopped. We were all grateful that the crisis had passed and he was restored to good humor and an interest in our individual troubles and attempts at creation.

That Saturday Kelly called me. "How's college?" I asked her.

"How would I know? My mother made me come home. She cancelled her last check and she called the dean of students and said I was needed here."

"What happened? Did somebody die?"

"She found out I was living with Mason."

"Did she come up without warning?"

"She was told. Guess who."

"He couldn't!" But I knew immediately that she had to be right.

Kelly's mother was determined to separate the couple. She would not lose her daughter, she kept saying.

"Don't send her away to another college," Mr. Danelli warned Mrs. Aimes. "She's only get in the same mess. Send her to the community college where I can keep an eye on her—and it will save you a bundle anyhow."

So Mason quit school too and they went off to Chicago, where he tried to get gigs playing someplace, anyplace and they both went to night school. Mason got a job in a 7-Eleven and Kelly waitressed. They lived in a one-room apartment near the L. When I took the bus to visit them, they were fighting a lot.

The first week in May Mr. Danelli came up to me as I was walking out of the school library and took hold of my arm just above the elbow. "Why don't you come up and see me some time? You haven't been in the office. I want to see what you've been producing."

I told him I was really busy, it being the end of my senior year, and I wouldn't have time for the *Signpost*. I suppose he understood, because he stopped saying hello in the hall.

The girls continue to come and go in the *Signpost* office and he still has enthusiasm for his favorites. I see him differently now, good for another ten years of sending us out to do the things he didn't and break the rules he can't and fight off his temptations. He finds himself equally betrayed in our successes as by our failures. But I worry about that daughter of his.

Do You Love Me?

Circa 1960

Oily night pads in. The city reeks. But it is chilly in the room under the eaves of the townhouse, where they pitch in bed. To her, Edmund feels all spines. He penetrates her like a question and she responds with her hips nervously, shallowly.

"I don't know if I love you." Edmund, whom nobody calls Ed, is sitting on the bed's edge, thinner than ever.

She shivers with sweat. "Should I leave? Go back to New York?"

"Of course not." Politely. "Don't be melodramatic."

"It's worse since we started sleeping together."

"Worse?" He shoots to his feet, reaching for his briefs. "What's worse? It's enough to make anyone nervous, tiptoe-ing around my parents' house."

"Why do we stay here then? Let's go someplace else."

"You said you liked them."

"I do. Especially your father. He's a dear."

He winces, misbuttoning his shirt. Waits for her to help him. In his angular face the grey eyes are set wide. They look past her, anticipating his flight down to the second floor.

Tossing on the cot after he has left, she hears dry voices, the ticking of glib excuses of the men who have borrowed and used her. Her fingers scrape the sheets. She is twenty-three and he is twenty-eight, an instructor who was her section man in philosophy when she was in college, but she is his instructor in bed. She shares herself with him as a winning argument. But he takes her gingerly, and afterward, it is as if sex were something he had stepped in.

After she graduated, they had run into each other in the coffee house she still frequented. They went out from time to time last winter and spring, evenings he had taken more seriously than she had. People said she was pretty; she danced well; there were always men. She had been astonished when he proposed she spend the summer with him in his parents' home. He said they would learn a great deal about each other without being committed to anything, that she would like Boston and find their home comfortable. He was thinking about marriage: that amazed her. Therefore she did not say No, but Maybe. She took him home with her by way of testing, but learned little except that he settled easily into a placid boredom.

Her photographer boyfriend dumped her for a mon-eyed girlfriend with a loft in SoHo. She stayed with friends, then other friends, sleeping on lumpy couches. She had imagined being an editor, making the delicate literary decisions she had been taught in college, but she was asked if she could type. She found a job so boring she would sometimes think she would die at her desk in the long mornings and longer afternoons. They started to talk at her about dressing differently. She called Edmund in Boston.

Now the house encloses her like an elbow. The house is as busy with a hundred concealed pursuits and escapes as a forest. His father talks to his mother; his mother talks to the Black maid. She and the mother give each other little electric shocks. The father is okay—scotch-and-water, the Maine woods in hunting season, the local *Globe* and the *New York Times*, and a blown wistfulness in his thick face. The mother is tall and dry. She seems to move with the sound of tissue paper.

Coming into Edmund's territory, she finds that whether they are to marry, whether he wants to, grows every day bigger and bigger. She rests in his hands like something inert.

Edmund lies in his ivory bedroom. He turns his cheek against his special firm pillow, drifting through his melancholy love for his married cousin Isabel—roses in waxy green paper, Limoges china. Soothing as his mother's hands in childhood fevers.

He feels her in her attic room pressing down on his head. Why did he bring her here? Often he cannot remember. Sometimes she resembles his dreams of the girl who will belong to him, but sometimes she grates. He is amused to think she was born in a Western where names are jokes, the town of Dogleg Bend where dust shimmies in the streets under a sky of mercury.

Once he went there with her. Her waitress mother, fat and messy, greeted her without surprise. Her younger sister seized her and they remained closeted for hours. She spoke to no one on the streets. She took him around a maze of overgrown fields and swaybacked houses, playing guide as if there were anything to be seen: that's where we lived the year I was ten. That's where my sister Jeannie and I used to fish on the sandbar. There's where the Massey boys caught me when I was coming from the diner, and when I yelled, they jumped up and down on my stomach. That's where I saw a wounded goose, in fall when they come over.

He has brought her to his family as a well-trained retriever will bring something puzzling to lay at his man's feet and wait, expectant. Is it good? Do we eat it?

By breakfast-time the heat has begun to rise, seeping into the shuttered windows. Her face, cool from sleep across the English marmalade and muffins and yesterday's flowers, seems young again, closed into itself. He wants to touch her.

His hearty father makes a joke about their wan morning faces. His mother suggests with buttery kindness that the girl's dress is somewhat short for the street. All eyes pluck at the seams of bright (too bright?) cotton. Do they know? Their hopeful politeness enwraps him. Yes, they would be glad to spread her on that maid's cot, to serve her up to ensure that he is whole and healthy. His mother has always read books on mind-repairing. "Son, I want you to feel free to bring your friends home." "Remember you have nothing to be shy about." "I've asked Nancy Bateman—you know the Batemans' adorable younger daughter?—to dinner Friday . . ."

He says, "Mother, Father, we're going to the cottage for a week. It's too hot here. It's unbearable."

Her eyes leap from their private shade, but she only takes more jam and teases his father. He knows, in deep thankfulness, that she is pleased and will reward him with an easy day. She will take his wrist in a hard grip and pull him off to play tourists in his own city. All day she will ask nothing. All day she will turn them into magic children from a story. He wants to push away from the table and hurry out with her.

They go to the cottage. Coming back from the cross-roads store with groceries, she looks at him beside her. She cannot imagine marriage. But she knows it is what makes a woman real, weights her to a name and place. That safe feeling she would seek walking in the old cemetery: names and dates neatly grouped in families, even the little babies accounted for. She wanted to get away as long as she can remember. But being a secretary is no better than being a waitress, except that her back and feet hurt less and her eyes hurt more.

He says, "I thought you'd be more struck by the town-house. We're proud of the wood paneling and the staircase. It dates from 1830."

But all houses impress her. All other dogs have equally big bones. Walking beside him she catches her breath as they come over a hill and the ocean stretches out into haze. She is surprised again how tall it is, how much sky it uses up. That blue yawn is her future. She will drown.

This cottage squats on the last dune, facing the sea. She puts down the groceries and sits at the white sea-blistered table. She sits still with concentration. On the table are shells and pebbles she has been collecting.

She says without inflection, "I packed my suitcase."

"I saw you. Why? How can you leave?"

"There's a bus that stops on the highway at four-ten, the woman at the crossroads store told me."

"Why? Where do you want to go? You quit your job."

She lays out the pebbles in circles. "You don't want me to stay, enough."

He sees himself returning to the city without her. The air will prickle with questions. Suppose after she leaves, he changes his mind and realizes he wants her? "Where will you go?" Her travel-worn suitcase with wheels that squeak stands at the door.

She picks sand from the ribs of a scallop shell. "New York? Maybe I'll go west. Maybe California."

Choosing a place so idly makes him dizzy. He sees her blown off like a grasshopper. People cannot just disappear. "By yourself?"

His tedious jealousy of tedious young men. She smiles. Her heart is chipping at her ribs. The road comes over the last dune fitted to its curved flank in a question mark. She does not dare turn from him to go inside and look at the clock. Will she really have to go? Will she have to get on that dirty bus and use up her last few dollars on a cheap motel? She concentrates on his bent head: want me! Want me, damn you. She is not sure how much money she has in her purse and wishes she had counted it in the bathroom.

He is staring at his knuckles, big for the thinness of his hands and bone-colored with clenching. "Do you love me?"

She turns her head. Her gaze strikes into his with a clinking, the stirring of a brittle wind chime. He is thinking about girls, the difficulty, the approaching, his shyness, the awkward phone calls with silences that open under him like crevasses in a glacier.

She is wondering what she is supposed to say. "What do you care?"

"I have to know."

His long milky face, pleading laugh, set of mismatched bones. He is gentle. If he does not touch her with passion, neither does he hurt her. That is very important, not to be hurt. "Of course I love you."

"Do you?" Once again he ducks to stare at his knuckles.

She must risk breaking the tension. She goes to read the clock.

"What time is it?" he calls.

She comes back to answer. "Five to four. I hope I haven't forgotten anything."

A strand of hair in the washbasin? Steel hands press on his shoulders: decide, decide. His father's voice, rising with the effort to contain his temper. "Squeeze the trigger, Edmund, squeeze it. Come on, it won't wait for you all day. Do it!" The rabbit bolted into the tall grass. In his relief he shot. His father strode away. Be a man, be a man. Pressure of steel hands.

He has always been fastidious not to give pain. "Let's walk down to the water."

She shakes her head. "Not enough time. I can't miss the bus accidentally, don't you see?" In New York it will be hot. She will call somebody. She will sleep on a couch, and the next day again she will go around to the temp agencies in whatever is still clean. Men will pester her on the street, men will buy her supper and expect to lay her as payment. "I can't sit here any longer waiting for you to decide if you love me—can I?" She claps the sand from her palms, hating herself for having listened to his quiet voice, for having given herself into his hands like a bag of laundry.

He cradles his head, elbowing aside the shells and pebbles. They move him, the sort of treasures a child might hoard. He feels wrong, not sure why. He hates the carelessness of men like his father, men in the fraternity of his college years whose act of power is to give pain. He does not know what he wants, only that everything is going away. She is about to walk off with that flimsy suitcase and leave him tangled here.

She reads his face—sullen, puzzled. He will let her go. Her skin crawls. One more defeat. "Well, want to walk me to the crossroads? It's time."

But he does not rise. "Stay."

Hope scalds her. She wants, wants so badly that surely she must win. "Why let it drag on?"

"You know it's hard for me to figure out what I feel sometimes. I'm slow to react. I can't just decide like that."

"You can tell if you love me. You could tell you wanted me here for the summer, before."

He is afraid, but of what? Her leaving? "But I do love you!" He breaks from his chair, snatches the suitcase from her. "I do love you. I want us to stay together." The words slam like a door he is finally through. He feels weak with relief. He has done the right thing. He too will have a wife. He will have a wife and children with his name.

"Then I'll stay." She stands quite still. That blue future gathers itself in a wave and goes crashing over her. I've won! she tells herself. Now I'll be safe. Now I'll belong. And I'll be ever so good to him. I'll never take another bus. I'll never sleep on somebody else's couch again.

But her spine is water and her hands curl up remembering that vertical house, his parents with their expectant eyes, his ivory bedroom with its air of sickroom. His thin arms fold around her in a tight but formal embrace like an up-ended box.

The Retreat

Circa 1970

Always the bedroom is dark. Oh, there are windows, two, onto a canyon echoing neighbors' sorrows and appliances. The crash of a bottle. A husband and wife tearing at each other. Children disemboweling a cat. The pelvic throb of mating cries, falsetto yowls over electric guitars reverberating like a permanent hangover. Noises pulse from other boxes.

Afternoon. Heat packed like grime into the sockets of her body, she lies prone. Let out early today because the air conditioning broke in the false moon of fluorescence and files, she came home and did not pause at the refuge of coffee shop where students sit in swirls of talk and where she sometimes sits pretending she is a student still. If you are a student people talk with you, they ask questions. If you are a working wife they look through you. She came home to clean the apartment thoroughly. Today she would set everything right.

She entered the dark, the summer sun fading into her skin. Their rooms felt packed with stale breath. On the cot that served as couch, the coverlet frowned wrinkles. On his desk her husband's work crouched waiting for him. Posters tacked to the walls look faded, outdated. Who cared about that band any longer? Not her. Then she wanted only to be swallowed into sleep. Fingers sunk into the pillow now she runs through clotted thickets hung with huge red flowers. The pursuing male, naked anyface, runs close behind. She stumbles. He overtakes and takes her. Memory of orgasm, the overtones from silence. She rises into shame. Kneels in her sweat scrubbing the roach-stained floor. When he comes home, it will be nice for him.

He wakes in the dark. Though the bedroom is always dark, night thickens it. Coming from a late seminar, he saw the white wafer of October moon, but it cannot enter here. Straightening his knife-blade back, he heaves the chilly air into his lungs. Peers into the dark. Hears only the wind scraping drifts of fallen leaves and discarded papers in the canyon between the apartments. Why should sweat slime him as if an army of frogs had crawled over his skin? Her hot body swamps his flank. The walls lean inward. He thrust free of the coil of sheets, gathering his pillow and the spread from the foot of the bed. As if he stood in a cave and looked out, at the corridor's end white moonlight pierces the bay window of the living room to freeze on the rug. She wakes, rolls on one round elbow to see him, pillow clasped to his shoulder, dragging the spread behind like a broken tail of a peacock.

"Where are you going?"

"The couch."

"Why?"

With the wincing shrub she knows too well, he ducks away. "I can't sleep." He stalks toward the white field that waits at tunnel's end. His side of the bed cools under her searching hand. In some unconscious way she has failed or offended him. She calls his name. The word fades.

Light comes down the corridor from the living room where he studies. One o'clock. She must get up at seven for work. The wind will freeze her as she waits for her bus, ice will enter her ankles. Kneeling naked and winter pale on the bed, she sees herself in the wavery mirror over the dresser that came with the apartment. He grunts distantly. She calls louder.

"What is it?" he says like a groan.

What? Me. Your wife you see as demanding. "When are you coming to bed?"

"When I finish. Go to sleep."

She weighs her breasts in her hands with a smile of derision. When I was a graduate student, I did finish. She had left after her masters to support him, as his family, as her family, as he himself expected. After all, a physicist is more important than an English doctoral student. And do I believe he will be different later? I feel disloyal judging him. I am not supposed to think this way. But he is never done and I am always waiting.

She puts on her only nightgown, pre-wedding extravagance in blush silk and lace, brushes her hair crackling. In the wavery mirror, she seems to be dissolving in her flimsy nightgown. Why should she be more attractive dressed in this thin strip of silk than standing as herself? A pierced unicorn, image of a tapestry she saw at the Cloisters in Manhattan with another man years before, looks over her shoulder from the wall. Her husband tacked it there. She is not the unicorn, blood bubbling on the ice-white flank and deflowered by pike and dogs. Her face fixed in a smile, she goes barefoot into the living room.

Afterward she sleeps curled toward him, relaxed, looking pleased. Afterward he sleeps too and dreams of a bleeding unicorn who stares at him with his mother's eyes. He grinds his teeth and groans. His out-flung arm strikes her. She wakes and leans to see him in his struggle. Her eyes drip hot as candlewax down her cheeks. Winning is losing and losing is losing too. Even in sleep they are chained together and she is dragged like a broken tail through his nightmares.

Whispering. Low sluttish whispers and a stench of fish. A cat scuttles past him with some live thing in its mouth. An old woman in black is watching him, and the beads of the portiere over her door click in her seeking hand. An open sewer dribbles down the winding stairs of street. Whispering again. Who? Awake at once, he sits up with a jagged hammering against his breastbone. No, not whispering. Just rain.

She stirs, far on her side of the gullied sheet. Just spring rain slithering down the windows, rain with a queasy smell of upturned earth. Something that should have been done has been forgotten. Something owed is coming due. His anxiety feels almost comfortable, accustomed. He knows that she is holding her breath like a silenced alarm, listening. To the rain? To his breathing?

He says, "You were out very late at your girlfriend's. What time did you get in?"

Pretending sleep, she imitates soft noises of coming to.

More loudly he asks, "What time did you come home? What were you doing?"

"Just talking. I didn't notice the time. Oh, hours ago."

Two on the green-eyed clock. He is quite sure if he reached out his hand, her hair would be wet, freshly wet, with the rain.

The window is open on the mild leafy night and the shade taps and taps in the small late spring wind. He rises, gathers his pillow, yanks the spread off. Awake beside him from his tossing and the churning of her own thoughts, she sits up on an elbow and watches him go dragging his bedding down the dark corridor toward the cot in the living room.

Tonight he accused her of being unfaithful, and she laughed. Faithful, unfaithful to what, she wonders. He does not believe she has been with her friend, talking. He withdraws, withholds, makes himself scarce to punish her. She is already moving in another direction. She watches him go, then stretches out again. And says nothing. She imagines a bed that will be all her own in a place that will be tiny but light and hers alone.

She has been making plans with her friend who knows a couple of available rentals. She made a list tonight. Saturday, the first day she doesn't work, she will look for that space behind some rented door.

What Remains

Intensely purple flowers in the shape of steeples appeared at the back fence of my vegetable garden last year. I didn't know where they came from. After a week, I looked them up in one of my gardening books. Loosestrife. Although some nurseries still sell it, it's widely condemned as an invasive weed. But it was pretty. I knew I would let it grow and then regret it in two years and spend several more trying to eradicate it. I've gone through this cycle before. But the flowers were attractive and lasted a long time in a vase.

The honey locust I planted outside my bedroom window the year I moved here with my then-husband, that gave me welcome light shade with its delicate leaves, was dying. In fear of it falling on the house in a nor'easter or hurricane, I had it cut down. Expensive, but what could I do? Underground it did not die but continued to sprout baby trees all over the place, even in the center strip of the driveway beside my little house. Its vitality amazed me. I cut them down but they simply pushed out of the ground in another place. Again, sometimes I let them be. But usually they died, as if the energy was only sufficient for a sapling but not nearly enough to make a tree.

My sister was sick with cancer of the small intestine. I didn't know what to think of all this fecundity. Was it a mad growth similar to what was eating her from the inside? Was it proof that something goes on after death? My sister Sandra was very sick 700 miles away in Buffalo. I couldn't move there. I work for a living and I'm glad to have two jobs. If I quit either, I could not survive. As it was, I had to do without health insurance for two years until the State mandated a nice cheap policy. Sandra had insurance. She had a better job than I do, but when she got cancer, they said she could no longer work enough hours to do the job and they let her go. It's lucky she had insurance, believe me.

I drove out to see her whenever I dared get away. I drove all night on Friday after work. That way I could spend Saturday and most of Sunday with her and then drive all night to get back for work on Monday. I drank a lot of coffee, even more than I usually do. Working two jobs, I try to stay caffeinated.

She'd finished another round of chemo four weeks before, so it sounded like a good time to visit. She would still be fagged out but able to spend time and talk. Sometimes when she was on chemo, she just wanted to sleep and I felt like I was more of a nuisance than a help. I brought her vegetables from my backyard garden. She liked that. She only wanted to eat organic. I thought it was a little late to worry about that, but if it made her feel better, why not?

I'm divorced for nine years, my son Rick finally moved out and is living with his girlfriend in Charlotte, North Carolina, and both our parents were dead. Basically my sister Sandra was the main person my life, the one I always talked with three evenings a week and emailed almost every day. My son sends me text messages it takes me five minutes to decipher. I hate text messages. They have no flavor. They could be sent by anybody. All those stupid emoticons. Smiley face. Frowny face. LOL. IMHP. I could be trying to communicate with a robot.

I thought Rick and I were close, especially after his

father took off with a massage therapist and moved to Arizona. I like Rick's girlfriend okay, but he has disappeared into that relationship. I suppose that's good. It took him long enough to settle down. But this was a time when I needed him. I have local friends, but working two jobs, I don't get to see a lot of them. We have an occasional brunch on Sundays or go to the movies or have a meal together in a moderately priced restaurant or just share a beer in my backyard, sitting in the Adirondack chairs that I bought when I was still married. But everybody's busy. Sheila still has the twins at home; Carlie is very married; Nita is having an affair with a landscaper who lives in West Roxbury. We all live in Roslindale. It's part of Boston but kind of separate. I live like most women my age, a bit tired, a bit shabby, a bit lonely, more than a bit worried. When I watch TV, which I admit I do most evenings, all the women seem so shiny and put together. If I get to wash my hair a couple times a week, that's the best I can do for upkeep. I've given up expecting Prince Charming to come by in a white convertible. I have my work outfits, a couple of dressy things that have lasted me for almost a decade. I treat my clothes well; I have to.

So I managed to get out half an hour early on Friday from the real estate office where I work in Dedham three days a week. My boss was showing a house and said she wouldn't be back. I had packed the old Ford with my suitcase, some veggies from the garden and was ready to head for Buffalo. I packed a sandwich to eat on the way and a thermos of coffee. It was September and still light when I passed Springfield on the Turnpike. Too bad I was driving into the sunset, so the flaws in my windshield almost blinded me, but I'm used to squinting and I never speed. I think my old car would fly apart if I tried.

Finally the damned sun sank into a cloudbank and I could take off my sunglasses, reach over and put on my regular glasses. Prescription bifocals and they cost me too much, but what can I do? I hate driving into the sun as much as I hate driving into other people's brights, but night driving is how I got to Sandra. I was hoping the doctor had given her news of remission after her CRI last week. They always took so long to give her results, as if she could think about anything else until she found out.

I was sorry to be driving through the Berkshires at night because the Mass Turnpike is pretty by day, but I had to make time. I called her just after I crossed into New York to let her know I'm arriving approximately when.

"Don't sit up for me. I know where the key is. I'll let myself in and get some shut eye on the couch."

"I'll open it up and put sheets on for you. I couldn't stay awake even if you wanted me to. I'll be glad to see you."

Like me, Sandra was divorced but she never had children. She worked for a ladies magazine and then various newspapers in the ad department, good pay and she liked the work. I always felt she had done much better than me. I went to college too at U Mass Boston, but I got married and had my son and never did have a professional job, the way Sandra had. I had a little girl baby too but she died of meningitis when she was only three. It broke my heart, but after that I poured everything into my son.

I took the key from under the pot of dead geraniums on her porch and let myself in. It was sad to see the dead flowers, Sandra had always loved geraniums, not the red ones but pastels. She had opened up the daybed for me and made it with sheets bright with umbrellas in various colors dancing across them. I assumed she was asleep, so I undressed, crept into bed and turned off the light. I was exhausted but all the coffee kept me awake until faint grey light was leaking through the windows.

I did sleep for a while until I heard her moving around in the kitchen. I jumped up then, put on my bathrobe and joined her. I did not like the way she looked, grey and much thinner than the last time I saw her, yet kind of puffy.

But I said, "You're looking better. What did the doctor say?"

She rose and opened a cabinet, took out kibble and shook it into three bowls. Two black sleek cats and one grey long-haired tabby were circling her feet, rubbing and make little noises. She got them settled and returned to the table.

"Tell me how you are?" I repeated.

She sat down at the table and was eating an apple, very slowly. She pointed toward the refrigerator. "Why don't you make yourself some eggs? I don't have bacon or sausage, but there's bread for toast."

"That's fine. Or I could just have cereal."

"In the cabinet there. It might be stale." She pushed her fine pale brown hair with its streak of grey out of her eyes. I was afraid her hair would have fallen out, but it just looked a bit lank. "Help yourself."

I ate the cereal with a banana. The cereal was stale, but I hadn't come all this way to eat breakfast. "So how are you doing?"

She put down the apple as if it had grown heavy. "The cancer has metastasized. It's in my liver."

"Can't they operate?"

"It's too far along." She looked into my eyes with hers that were so like my own. "I'm dying, sis. They give me maybe two months. I'm putting my affairs in order."

"Are you sure there's nothing can be done? Did you get a second opinion? In Boston, there's great doctors."

"It's the way it is." She picked up the apple and looked at it. "There are things that must be settled."

I put down my spoon. My stomach felt filled with cement. I could not swallow. "Don't they offer any hope?"

She shook her head. "I'm too far gone."

"Why aren't you in the hospital?"

"I don't want to die there. It would all be pain for nothing. In five days I go into hospice. It's all arranged."

"Why didn't you tell me? You could come and stay with me."

"In the hospice they can give me morphine for the pain. It's settled . . . but so much isn't. I put the house on the market. I reduced the price until it sold. I'm leaving the money to you, after my bills are paid. There won't be much but maybe it will help."

"You don't have to do that."

"I want to. Who else would I leave it to? Besides, I'm going to ask you a favor and that will help pay for it."

"Anything." Perhaps to arrange her funeral or her burial? I blinked back the burning in my eyes. To cry felt self-indulgent. She was being so brave and practical.

"Come into my bedroom." She walked so slowly it took us five minutes just to cross the kitchen and pass through the dining room to her bedroom. It smelled like a sickroom, of medicine and decay. My eyes burned with tears I held back. I snuffled as quietly as I could. I longed to hug her but was afraid it would be painful for her frail body.

She opened a jewelry box on her vanity. "Here's my diamond ring. It ought to be worth something. And solitaire earrings, two karats. I had them appraised. You should get a couple of thousand for them, at least. These are real pearls. You might want to keep them. You should go through and see if there's anything else you might like. The rest is just costume jewelry. I gave a bunch to my cleaning lady." She held the pearls to the light, almost caressing them, then dropped them warm from her touch into my palm.

"Whatever you want." I was never one for jewelry. I suppose I could give the pearls to Rick's girlfriend. Or maybe Nita would like them. Yet I was not sure I would be able to give away anything that had belonged to Sandra. Even if I never wore those pearls, they had touched her skin often and they retained some essence of her. The diamonds meant less to her. I'd sell or pawn them as she suggested.

"You should look through my closet. See if there's anything that might fit you. I'm pretty sure my cashmere winter coat will. I bought it big so I could wear sweaters or suit jackets under it."

"Sandra, stop! I want you, not all this stuff."

"I'm going into hospice and the people who bought the house will be moving in shortly afterward. I'm leaving the furniture. They can do with it whatever they decide."

She insisted I go through her closet and gave me a suitcase with wheels, the sort of thing people who travel a lot own. I'm too heavy for most of her things—not that I'm fat, just broader than Sandra ever was. I ended up with some oversized sweaters, the coat, a couple of jackets and a silk bathrobe. What would I ever do with a silk robe? It brought home to me how different our lives had been.

She insisted I take a food processor and some fancy pots, a peacock vase she was proud of, a platter in the shape of a fish, her silverware. Then at last she sank into a chair in the living room. "If there's anything else you see that you want, just take it."

I could not bear it. I shook my head.

"Please look around. It makes me sad to think of strangers throwing all my nice things out, giving them to the Salvation Army or whatever . . . Now for the favor."

The big grey tabby had climbed in her lap and she was petting it absently. "I want you to take the cats. If you don't, they'll go to the shelter and be killed. I can't stand that. I just can't."

"Three cats? But I work two jobs. I'm not around much."

"They keep each other company. They kept me company. They've been loyal friends to me no matter how ill I became. I cannot send them to be executed just because I'm dying. Will you do this for me?" Her voice rose. "Please!"

I couldn't imagine what I'd do with three cats, but I said, "Of course. Just tell me what they need."

Tears crept down her face and I found myself weeping along with her. We sat facing each other, both with tears rolling down our faces. I hated the thought that this might be the last time I ever saw my sister.

Visibly she pulled herself together, sitting up, still stroking the grey tabby. "We'll load their scratching post, their litter box, their toys and food. Mitzi and Cleo—the two blacks—they go in one carrying case. Merlin goes in his own case."

So Sunday around two I loaded my car with various clothes, a lamp she pressed on me, the pots, the dishes, a quilt and all the accoutrements of three cats who began to yowl piteously as soon as they were loaded into their carrying cases. Merlin had to be dragged out from under her bed.

All seven hundred miles back to Roslindale, they yowled. I had to pull over a couple of times because my tears blinded me. Every mile, every hour took me farther from Sandra. I was tempted to turn around and call in sick, but I knew she really did not want me there. As she kept saying, she had a lot to settle before she went into the hospice.

When I brought them in, the two black cats ran away terrified into nether reaches of my smallish house. Merlin stood his ground and growled at me. I put down food for them in the bowls she had packed, put the litter box in my bathroom and filled it, put down water, set up their scratching pad. I did not see the black cats again but all the food was gone in the morning.

I called Sandra to give a report. By evening, all the cats came out of hiding and stood waiting for food. They would not let me touch them, but they ate, they used the litter box, and that night, Merlin climbed into my bed and lay against me. He even began to purr. It was oddly comforting. I felt as if the four of us were in mourning. Perhaps we could mourn together.

I had a lot to learn about cats. If I didn't scoop out their leavings from the litter boxes every morning, they deposited little complaints on the bathroom rug. Each of them had different food habits, and Merlin had to be fed up on the kitchen counter away from the girls, or he would raid their dishes. If I didn't play with them, they'd make games of knocking things over and chasing each other around the house at night. I took a book out of the library on cat behavior. It said cats could be trained, but I found that I could be trained far more easily.

A year has passed since Sandra died. I flew back for her funeral. Carlie fed the cats. I have no reason to go to Buffalo again. The money from the house and the jewelry I keep in the bank for emergencies. Me and my five cats live happily together. Friends pity me silently, but I know better. I got one more from the MSPCA, an orange three-year old male I call Pumpkin. Then somebody dumped a skinny female on my porch in a box from a liquor store. She turned out to be pregnant, but the vet said she was too starved to carry the kittens to term. No problem with an abortion for a cat. My new vet is a 70-year-old guy who loves animals. When I commented on the abortion, he laughed and said that when he started to practice, abortions were illegal for women but perfectly fine for cats. I named her Lucky. I don't think she stopped eating for two months.

When I come home from work, they greet me at the door. We dine together. We watch TV. Each cat has a specific place in my bed. They purr me to sleep and they wake me in the morning. Each one is a strong personality; each is affectionate with me and they get along pretty well with each other. They are better company than my husband ever was. I'm cutting back on my gardening to spend time with them. They're more entertaining. I am letting the loosestrife take over that bed and letting the locust babies grow (except in the driveway). I miss my sister and probably always will. I still work two jobs, I am often exhausted, I am still shabby and somewhat overweight and without male companionship, but I am no longer lonely. I have a family of five—and perhaps I will adopt more. I lost my sister and I still miss her desperately, but she left me a destiny: the cat lady of my neighborhood in Roslindale. It's something that works for me. I think she knew what she was doing when she bequeathed me her cats. We had always taken care of each other and now I have a little family to fuss over.

The Border

Circa 1967

She drove, not too fast, never over the speed limit but not too slowly either—the important thing was not to attract attention. She had the car radio on to the new album the Beatles had just put out, *Revolver*. The DJ was playing it all the way through with interruptions for acne medication, shampoo and beer commercials. She would have liked to turn it up to help her stay awake, but if she did, he might wake up. In the backseat, the man was still sleeping, occasionally moaning or cursing or grunting. It was better when he was asleep. Awake, he made her nervous.

She admired the vets against the war, admired those like her charge who refused to go back. The feds would call him a deserter but she saw him as someone driven by guilt and courage into an unknown life, where he could only hope for shelter—once she got him across the border. But he was a little scary, she admitted to herself. She knew that almost all of them, the deserters she helped, not the ones who were avoiding the draft, had serious drug problems and sometimes seemed crazed. Her job was just to get him to Canada tonight. She had done this five times before: three times for men fleeing the draft—whose number had been called up—and twice before tonight for guys who simply could not bear to go back to Vietnam.

She was a good choice because she was a woman, her comrades in the anti-war movement said, and because she had an old Volvo. Activists who lived in Manhattan were unlikely to own cars—it was like having an elephant for a pet. Where could you keep it that didn't cost more than your rent? But she had an apartment in the basement of a brownstone in Park Slope and she could park on the street. The car had belonged to her husband, but when she got too involved in the Movement and he left, he gave her the old car. Bought himself a newer one. Got himself a newer squeeze who didn't drive to Canada in the middle of the night risking arrest. She had two lovers, but neither of them lived with her. One was better in bed and the other was better out of bed; together they made one good boyfriend. After all, nobody could satisfy all of another person's needs and desires. Better to patch things together and blunder on. Her ex hadn't been good either way the last couple of years.

He was beginning to stir in the back seat and she was getting low on gas. They were just across the border into Vermont, still on 91. She'd watch for a station open twenty-four hours, probably a truck stop. She had to pee anyhow. All that coffee was on its way through her. When she did one of these runs to Canada, she tanked up, since she wanted to arrive around dawn near the border. Few people awake and stirring, little traffic but visibility okay.

Her usual Movement job was draft counseling. That was more comfortable. She'd sit across a table in the Peace and Freedom office or if the client—she called them clients—was not comfortable going there, she'd meet them in a coffee shop. She'd ask, "How much do you want to stay out of Vietnam? Because if you really want to, I can tell you how to fail your physical and be let go. But if you don't want it desperately enough, you won't do what you have to." She explained how to act gay; how to act crazy; how to shock enough to get out. Often she could tell by the man or boy's reaction to her suggestions if the guy had the courage or the willingness to act against all convention and acceptable behavior. If a guy wanted to avoid the draft enough, she could help. By the time they left, she had a pretty good idea if they were going into the meat grinder. She could not force them to act on her scenarios. She did not try to talk them into it. It had to be their own choice. But sometimes she wanted to weep. Come on, she pleaded silently, an hour of shameless behavior or walking into the jungle to kill or be killed in somebody else's country where you don't speak the language, don't know the customs, don't belong. Come back with trauma and drug habits you can't deal with. Destroy your family. Be haunted the rest of your life. Please cross the line of acceptable behavior and save your life.

His voice broke her out of her reverie. "No," she answered. "We have many miles to go, all the way north through Vermont to the border. I'm watching for an open station for gas." She glanced at him, his knees drawn up toward his belly as if to protect it. He was lanky and thin and, of course, nervous.

When she saw the lights for an open truck stop, she took the ramp. After getting gas, she pulled into a spot. She had to use the bathroom and so did he. She hoped he looked normal. He had been wearing fatigues when they met, but she had provided him with civilian clothing that almost fit. They collected clothes at rummage sales kept in a box in the office.

He returned smoking and got into the front seat. "Do they have American cigarettes in Canada?"

"I don't know . . . I'd imagine so, but I don't smoke." She had stopped when her husband left. It saved money and a cough she had developed scared her. Now his smoke bothered her, but she suspected it would be even tenser if she asked him not to. Instead she cracked her window about an inch.

"If you're going to keep that fucking window open, turn on the heat."

"The cold helps keep me awake. Alert. The heater doesn't work well. I actually have it on."

He grunted. "You should get it fixed. Damn cold tonight."

"The guy in the garage said it had to be replaced, but this is an old car and parts are hard to come by." And she didn't have the money. In the Movement, many things came free: her dentist, her doctor didn't charge her. But the mechanic did.

He nodded and was silent for maybe fifteen minutes. Then he put his hand on her knee. "I'm beat. Want to stop at a motel? We could drive on after we take it easy, what do you say? Have a little fun."

"I have to work tomorrow. Have to be back before nine."

His hand began to work its way upward. She grabbed it and the car swerved. "I'm married, if you didn't notice." With men she didn't know, she put on her old wedding ring. It felt clumsy and bothered her in a minor way, its unaccustomed pressure on her finger reminding her of what she preferred to forget.

"Okay, okay. Don't drive into a ditch." He took his hand away and lit another cigarette from the stub in his mouth. Then he turned the radio louder. She was glad of that. It avoided having to talk. That passed an hour. Then the DJ changed and it was '50s songs she hated. Obviously so did he, because he shut the radio off. She had to make conversation. She noticed he had a nervous tic of scratching the back of his hands. They looked raw.

"Where are you from, originally?"

"Marquette. That's in the Upper Peninsula."

Michigan. She knew that much, even though she'd grown up in Rochester, New York. "They say you're born on skis."

He gave a brief snort of a laugh. "Yeah. You'd think I'd be used to the cold. I guess I was. But not anymore."

"Do you wish you could go back home?"

He was silent for a bit. "Yeah. My folks are there. Three brothers, two sisters and my ma."

"Where's your father?"

"Dead. Mining accident." He turned to stare out the side window into the darkness.

"A mine explosion?"

"You're thinking of coal mines. This is an open mine. A truck backed over him."

"I'm so sorry. That's awful."

"I think he was too hung over to hear it coming." He shrugged. "I was seven. I barely remember him. Just bits and pieces." He was silent for a bit and she tried to think of something less painful to ask. Then he shook his head. "That's when we moved to Marquette from near the mine. Mom got a job cleaning. She held the family together."

A police car was sitting on the side of the highway. She slowed down a little more, watching in the rear view mirror until it was out of sight.

She didn't really like to learn much about the guys she ferried. If she got to know them, she would worry what they were going to do in Canada, how it would work out for them, how they would manage never seeing their families again, how they would make a living. The more real she let them become, the more they would nibble at her brain, worrying, wondering. Once she drove off, she would never hear of them again, unless something went terribly wrong and they appeared in the newspaper or on the evening news. An occasional one couldn't take the isolation, the strangeness of it all and tried to come back. Usually they were caught. But his suggestion of a motel had unnerved her and she thought it safest to keep him talking. She thought of it as grounding him, giving him context, keeping him calm and distracted.

"What made you join the Army? Were you drafted?"

"My number came up. My brother Nolan already went, but he's a mechanic so he just works on trucks and jeeps and stuff. Sandy, my oldest bro, he's married with two kids and he's safe. Neil has a funny heart, like it skips beats, so they didn't take him. I wished I had that, I guess."

Atrial fibrillation? "Which one are you closest to?"

"Neil. Cause he's just a year and a half younger. Always looked out for him at school. So he wouldn't get beat up, you know. He was never no good at sports."

"What did you play?"

"Basketball and track. I was good at sprinting. Came in second in a hundred-yard dash in all state."

She was beginning to taste her fatigue, bile in the mouth. Her eyelids felt swollen and heavy. She had eaten a hasty supper at six and her stomach was growling, but she did not want to risk stopping in a well-lighted place. Best to keep going. His head lolling on his shoulder, he slumped in his seat, dozing, waking, dozing again.

"How much farther?"

"Another hour will do it."

In the east, the sky was streaked with grey. The dark was thinner, more watery-looking. About the only traffic were trucks also bound for Canada. "Do you speak French?" she asked him, already sure of the answer.

"French? No. Why?" He shook his head rapidly to wake himself.

"They speak French in Quebec. So head west to Toronto. Get into Ontario, anyhow."

"I was thinking about Windsor. It's right across the river from Detroit. Always looked neat and clean when I saw it."

"That's a long way. And too near the border. That's a major crossing. Toronto is better. There's guys like you there. They'll help you."

He was silent, staring out the side window. Perhaps the

realization was hitting him how alone he would be in a strange country. She tried not to think about it. Her job was just to get him across the border safely.

"We get off the interstate here." She used Derby Line, where the border ran down the main street. They got stuck behind a slow logging truck but then he turned off and she could hurry again. Her hands had begun to turn clammy on the wheel. She always had visions in her head of the old Volvo breaking down on one of these roads and she and her charge ending up in police custody. It had begun lightly snowing, just a few dry desultory flakes as if the sky had dandruff. A police car with lights flashing had somebody just before Derby Line. She checked her speedometer. Just under the speed limit. Still she couldn't bring herself to speak until she stopped watching for that cop in her rear view mirror.

"Now, what's your name?"

He started to say his real name and she interrupted, "Your traveling name."

"James Royce . . . Makes me feel like I'm in a spy movie."

"Why are you in Canada?"

"I'm going to Manitoba to see my aunt who married a Canadian."

"Where in Manitoba?"

"Winna something or other."

"Winnipeg."

"Are you a teacher or something?"

She grimaced. "I'm the person who's trying to get you into safety."

"Safety . . ." He thought about that, looking out the window again. The darkness was grainier. She hoped the snow would hold off. Footprints in new snow worried her. "I don't believe in that anymore."

They were on the outskirts of Derby Line now. A few lights in houses. Two cars passed them, but mostly it was deserted. She turned onto a side street, turned out her lights and rolled to a stop. "Go ahead. Just keep walking. There's a line and when you cross it, you're in Canada. There's a bus that comes through at ten and stops at the coffee shop. We've given you enough Canadian money. Try not to talk much so you don't give yourself away as American, but ask the driver to let you off for the bus to Montreal. This bus stops everyplace. Takes a long time. Try to sleep. You take it to where you can change for Montreal. Then take a bus to Toronto." She reached for her purse. "Here's the phone number of a contact in Montreal. You can stay with her for the night and she'll take you to the bus in the morning. And here's the address of help in Toronto, a group set up for guys like you to get you settled."

She waited till he nodded. He seemed reluctant to get out of the car. She patted his shoulder. "Best to get going before it turns light or starts to really snow. No one's around yet. Just walk quickly and turn left at the fourth street. The coffee house opens at six. That's half an hour. You can get something to eat there."

He opened the car door, turned and stared at her. "Guess I won't see you again."

"I hope not. That'd mean trouble for both of us."

He laughed. "I seen enough trouble to last me a lifetime, if I live that long." Still he stood looking at her. "Guess I should thank you."

"Just get moving and stay safe. I appreciate what you're doing."

"Nobody else I know would." Finally he turned and strode off, the knapsack they had given him slung on his back. She sat in the dark car watching him until he had crossed the border and kept walking until she could no longer see him. She felt sad, empty and relieved at once. Into the unknown he walked. Well, she better get out of here before someone wondered what she was doing. She turned the ignition and the car coughed and died. Her heart skipped and she thought of his safe brother. Neil? She waited a moment so she wouldn't flood the old engine and tried again and this time it started. She turned around carefully, thankful for the little car's tight turning radius. Then she headed out of the village. She fished a candy bar out of her purse, saved for this occasion and bit off pieces while she drove carefully toward the entrance to the interstate. The cop who had lurked near the ramp was gone. By the time she entered the interstate, it was snowing harder and soon the plows were out. It would be a slow trip. When she had gone a safe distance, she would stop for breakfast. She imagined him waiting for the bus and hoped he would not be obvious to anyone. She had used that village several times, scouting it beforehand. She could no longer help him, whatever happened. All she could do for those guys who became briefly her charges was to guide them to the border, see them across and then abandon them to whatever destiny they could create or blunder into on the other side. He was not the first and would not be the last. She owed her help, the risk she took, to the ones who decided not to fight. It cost her a day of prep and an all night and half a day drive; it cost those she ferried the rest of their lives. If you wanted to stop the war, this was one of the things you just did again and again.

I Had a Friend

I had a friend, Simon. He was big, almost bearlike, on the clumsy side with dark hair that flopped over his forehead. He was good looking but thought himself ugly. Something had damaged him already in his mid-twenties.

We worked together against the Vietnam War, against the draft, against imperial ambitions, against racism. We made a good team. We had both tried to work with other people but found ourselves undervalued, run over, our ideas never really considered—me because of being a woman and Simon because he was not an alpha male. We listened to each other. We wrote with me at the typewriter and him pacing behind me. It was a relationship of equals, comfortable for both. We went to demonstrations together and I felt a little protected with his powerful body beside me. I am still proud of what we did together. But in those days, I had multiple emotional and sexual relationships. Sex came easily to me and I enjoyed it. My affections were readily engaged without being possessive.

He grew obsessive. He demanded more and more attention. He resented my other relationships and insulted my friends. Once he threw one of those huge old office typewriters across the office where our group worked, narrowly missing one of my lovers. Another time when I was dancing at a party, he punched my partner, knocking him down. I thought his jealousy might quiet down if we were lovers and suggested it to him one afternoon when we had finished the pamphlet we were writing for a demonstration against the CIA. But he could not make love to me. He was impotent with me and that made him angry. His anger was terrifying. I withdrew a bit and so did he. We could no longer work together. That made me sad, but I moved on to work with others on different projects in different ways. I was a good organizer in those days.

Simon tried to work with several other activists, but he could not mesh his creativity, his drive, his ideas with theirs. Finally he withdrew from politics. He became a carpenter. He said that working with his hands was more honest than working with words. He made furniture. It was ugly. His bookcases leaned to one side. His chairs wobbled. His tables were untrustworthy. We got back in touch socially but that was all. He seemed to have fully recovered from his obsession with me, although he did present me with a lopsided bookcase.

Six months later he found G-d, an Orthodox Jewish god, male, frowning like a storm cloud. He grew a beard and let his sideburns grow, hoping for *peyeses*. He prayed loudly morning, afternoon and night and joined a *shul* with a charismatic rabbi. He would not eat in restaurants unless they were kosher. I served him swordfish but it was not kosher enough and he shoved his plate away. He tried to get me to dress more modestly—without success. He said his blessings every five minutes. I grew up with an Orthodox *bobbelah* who gave me my religious education, but my Hannah was a pagan compared to him.

I left New York for several months. When I returned, the beard was gone and he had a new girlfriend who was not Jewish. She was the blond perky suburban daughter of a successful real estate entrepreneur. They got engaged quickly and her father brought him into his business. For several months, all he could talk about was flipping houses and developing malls. I found him a total bore and avoided him, didn't return his calls. His interest in real estate and his engagement ended abruptly. A period of heavy drinking and drug use followed. He was often incoherent. He wept on my sofa and fell asleep face down.

He went back to school, having talked his parents into funding a graduate degree in psychology so he could become a therapist. He freely analyzed my problems over an Indian restaurant meal. He said he was coming to understand that I had been a replacement for his unhealthy love for his mother. Now all was clear to him. Mental health was the most important thing in the world. If we could all face our inner conflicts, there would be no war, no racism, no misery. My problem was that I felt unloved and replaced true commitment with promiscuity. He wondered if he shouldn't take a medical degree instead and then study psychoanalysis. He had a wonderful new psychiatrist. He was, he said, no longer self-medicating. His doctor had him on a new antidepressant that was working wonders for him. I hoped so. His period of heavy drugging had scared me. In all Simon's transformations, he was inherently lovable—something sweet and at the same time desperate in all his attempts.

I can sound flippant and above it all with his changes, but in truth I still cared about him and I hoped he would settle into something that made him happier or at least more engaged for the long run. I still felt guilty about having let him try a sexual relationship as a means of quieting his jealousy so he'd stop making scenes. I had offered myself to him as a sort of sop to make him behave in public. I wondered if only I hadn't done so, would we still be working together—a time he had felt fulfilled. I had not yet learned I could not be a sort of sexual mustard plaster to the sad and repressed.

I left New York in the early '70s when many politicos and hippies were moving to the country, including me. I still had many friends and attachments in the city, so I went back and forth every couple of months. The next time I saw him, he had shaved his head and wore loose saffron robes. He told me he was meditating daily, up to two hours at a time. He was fasting once a week. His mind was clear at last. He was now a vegan, so as not to injure any living thing. He was moving, too—to Sedona to be with his new guru. "I've been too materialistic. I want to enrich my soul, to live purely. I'm seeking my spiritual center. I need to be in a community that supports my evolving consciousness."

After that I lost touch with him for over a decade. I thought of him sometimes. I had a photo I had taken of him at a be-in in Central Park where he was lounging on the grass like a big overgrown puppy, smiling, relaxed, momentarily at peace. I could remember that day vividly, like a Medieval Fair come alive, the colors, the wild clothes, the music, the dancing, all spontaneous—and the smoke from maryjane. It was from the time we worked together, a time when he smiled often and was able to enjoy his life at least sometimes. A friend who'd been underground and gone to prison ran into him after she was free. He was still seeking fulfillment, as if seven years had not passed since they met. She shook her head in disbelief. He was making freeform artistic videos.

As I was about to go to bed one evening, already in my bathrobe with my hair braided, the phone rang. It was a friend I had stayed in touch with from my New York era. "Do you remember Simon?"

"Sure, though I haven't seen him in ten years. What's he into now?"

A silence. "He killed himself two days ago."

"Where?" A stupid question that filled in for "Why" and so much else.

"Madison. He was back in school in computer science but he couldn't seem to get into his thesis—some kind of computer language he was creating. The woman he was living with said he had been very depressed. He kept writing letters to old friends and tearing them up. She didn't think he'd mailed any."

"How did he do it?" Why do we always ask that about a death?

"He hung himself in his bedroom."

There would be a memorial in Madison but it was at a time I was already booked on a flight to London for a women's conference, so I could not attend. This is my memorial for a friend I lost, who lost himself though he tried again and again and again to fill an emptiness that tormented him. Memory is all that I have of him now.

Ring around the Kleinbottle

The matter began simply enough, when Cam and Vicki lost their roommate Janice. Janice moved out when she broke off her engagement to Allen Miner, a clever fellow who works in market research. Janice took an extended vacation and then set up in a studio by herself. I knew Janice from our mutual gym and a couple of coffees together, but I'd never met her roommates. Winning back my freedom in court recently had cost me so much I answered their ad and was glad to move into the spacious apartment in a 1920s-era brick apartment house. The living room was light, with a worn parquet floor and we each had our room. Vicki paid a little less than Cam and I since she had the ex-maid's room off the kitchen. Being three years older than Cam and seven years older than Vicki, I was determined not to play mama to them. Not my style.

A few weeks after I moved in, I saw Cam climbing out of Allen's Miata out front. So the next evening as we puttered around the kitchen, I said, "Guess it's lucky Janice moved out. Might be a bit awkward otherwise."

"What do you mean?" Cam is naturally defensive. She dresses to underplay her figure. Her face is gentle and sprinkled with freckles, her hair a natural light redhead—almost orange. Naturally soft-spoken, she has a stiff protective manner.

"With you seeing Allen. He got over Janice fast."

"You're misinterpreting." Her voice was husky with rebuke. "He's upset and he needs to talk with someone. He wants to patch things up with her, but Janice won't take his calls."

"So you're consoling him."

"Eve, I'm listening, that's all. While he was seeing Janice, I barely knew him, but I'm learning he's one of the good ones. Janice really hurt him."

Cam works for a pharmaceutical company torturing rats and bunnies. She'd be much happier as a social worker or a counselor. We lunched together last week—I'm the personnel director in a computer hosting and repair company with offices not that far from where Cam works. When I went to fetch her, she was all white-coated with her face bolted shut pretending to be a scientist. She's an oversensitive type who likes to act detached, even stolid, but I'm not fooled. In her veins runs butterscotch syrup. So I wasn't surprised when consoling Allen settled in to a full-time job. She told me she'd been engaged to a specialist in the army but when his deployment in Afghanistan ended, he broke things off with her almost without explanation. She said he had changed completely. She was convinced she had somehow failed him. Yet she seemed to be the wounded one.

Finally readjusting Allen needed all night. Vicki came bursting into my room Sunday morning—Vicki always explodes through doors. She's long-legged and thin only because she jumps around too much for the fat to settle, because she eats more than Cam and I put together. She's a year out of community college, working as a secretary. I can imagine her mixing up the files one day because she feels sorry for the poor neglected ones in the back. "Cam's not back!"

"Good. Been waiting for that."

"But with Allen? How could she?

"Why, is he a known eunuch?"

"He's still in love with Janice."

"That doesn't mean birdseed at one in the morning."

"I just don't want her to get hurt."

When Cam walked in, Vicki was waiting like an under-age mommy. "Where were you?"

Cam yawned broadly. "At Allen's, of course."

"About time you two made it," I said.

"Take it easy, Eve. We talked till Allen was too tired to drive me home, so I stayed."

"And you're telling me you slept like two babes in the woods?"

Cam shook her head. "Like two friends on a mattress."

Next weekend, Cam announced she was off to Springfield where she grew up, to take part in her cousin's wedding as a bridesmaid in a hideous fuchsia gown. "Must you go?" Vicki whined.

"Must. What's wrong, pet?"

"It's my twenty-first birthday Friday night. Guess I'll go down to the liquor store on the corner, flash my ID and buy a bottle of cheap wine."

The upshot was that Cam spoke to Allen, he took Vicki out and then there were two of them ministering to his sorrows. He was always on the stairs picking up one in his little sports car or bringing the other back. What with visiting his married friends, accompanying him to parties and movies and concerts and plays, bird-watching with him on weekends (you'd be surprised how quickly two bright women can learn to identify birds they had never noticed or heard the names of a month before), their lives seemed complete. Neither of them had dated anyone else since Allen had begun to occupy them. He paid for all this entertainment, since he earned quite handsomely. While they were comforting Allen, I must have gone through about five guys I met online.

I kept hearing lectures on Allen's character and habits. Over takeout Thai, Vicki foamed, "Even if he is older, he isn't boring and stuck. He believes like me the important thing is being as alive as you can be, not burying your feelings under a lot of dead words."

"He's a big believer in honesty, so I'm told."

"He's tremendously spontaneous. We do the wildest things on the spur of the moment, like inventing cocktails with all the stuff in his liquor cabinet, like taking off our clothes and jumping into the fountain by the library. We stole a parking meter last week but we couldn't get it open. Don't tell Cam! It's in his closet."

I noticed that Cam had begun to cook for him. Still, she addressed Vicki Monday at supper when Allen had his regular meeting at work. "I'm worried we're becoming too dependent on him."

"In what way?

In every way, I wanted to say, but kept my silence. "Someday Allen is going to resume his life. He's a wonderful person but we shouldn't let him become too important to us."

"I think you can never really hurt yourself by giving to someone." Vicki was straddling a chair, all earnest with her hungry kitten face.

"I envy you for believing that," Cam said, sighing heavily.

That Saturday, I was glad I moved in and that Cam was sitting out that evening while Allen took Vicki to the concert of a rock band she adored. My final papers had arrived Friday. I was glad to sit and drink with another woman, nothing at issue except the booze and whatever you felt like getting off your chest.

"I'm afraid I'm becoming fond of Allen. He's really a good person—serious, responsible, not like the usual men I meet. He's a true adult—you know how rare that is?"

"Do I!" I was thinking of my ex with his video games

and secret online porn. "American men don't grow up till fifty, and by then, who wants them?"

"Allen isn't like that. He's been through a lot, but it hasn't made him bitter. He listens when I talk—god, how long as it been since a man actually listened to me instead of counting seconds till they try to score."

"Sounds . . . fine." I was lying on the floor with my head on a couch pillow. Her voice seems to rise and sink.

"I think he's fond of me too." She paused, staring at her hands. "He's been . . . affectionate lately. He wants a deep and lasting relationship with a woman. But neither of us is about to rush into anything without being sure . . . I'm babbling and you're falling asleep." She sat up, holding herself across her breasts. "I don't feel jealous of Vicki—she's so young. She makes him laugh. He'd never take advantage of her."

I woke late Sunday a bit hung over. It's a long time since I let somebody drink me under the table. Cam can sure hold it. Vicki came prancing into my room. "Last night was so real! I don't want to make Cam jealous though she'll have to get wise to it sometime. We drove to the lakeshore. I dared him and we went wading. The water was so cold, it hurt but it felt great too! He told me I looked like a water nymph, whatever that is, and then he kissed me." Vicki didn't just speak, she vibrated.

I groaned. "Could you speak a little more softly?"

"Cam's in the basement doing laundry. She won't hear. This is just our secret . . . He let me drive the Miata back to his place. Then . . . we made it . . . I don't mean to fuss, but he doesn't do anything he doesn't mean . . . So we're lovers now. But I won't interfere with his friendship with Cam. It's just so different."

The next week was jolly. Each was telling me how nicely she thought her relationship with Allen was progressing, and I was beginning to wonder about him.

He was a friendly little guy with bright squirrel eyes, a thin mobile face and slightly receded hairline. The situation was hard to size up, for while I was getting a blow by blow from Vicky, Cam was her usual tightlipped self.

"Do you think I'm too defensive?" she asked me. "That I'm too closed off with people I care about?"

"Not particularly. Why?"

"I suppose I'm afraid of getting hurt again."

"Who's been handing you a line about your defenses?"

"It's that just Allen and I were talking. He says I don't let anyone really close." She gave me a half ashamed smile.

Presumably Cam was still worrying about her defenses when Vicki decided to spill about how she and Allen were lovers now and it was just great.

"Really?" Cam managed to sound only curious, but her fists were clenched. "Well, he must be over Janice at last."

"This doesn't mean it'll interfere with your friendship. Really!"

"I suppose he'll tell me about it tomorrow. Should I act surprised?"

"Your call." Vicki hopped up and paced as if she could not contain herself. "I've never really been in love before. I thought so, but this shows me that was just infatuation. I want to keep him warm at night and take care of him and remind him of things he's forgotten."

If we thought things were settled, we were dreaming. Allen didn't call Vicki Sunday or Monday, and by Tuesday, she was frantic. We suggested she call him, but she refused, huddling on the couch with her arms broken out in a nervous rash, angular as a ball of spikes. Cam was puzzled. Allen had said nothing about Vicki, she confided, but had given her another lecture on her defenses. After work on Wednesday, Vicki stuffed a few clothes into a duffle bag and went to stay with a friend from work. She said she was sick of waiting for him to call and shut off her cell.

I was doing my nails when the phone started ringing. "Hello, can I speak with Cam?"

"She's out. An emergency at work—sick bunny or something."

"How about Vicki?"

"She's not in either." He didn't ask where she was; I kept quiet.

"Allen here. And this is the third roommate, Eve, right? I couldn't mistake your voice. Black velvet."

"More like burlap, I've been told. Vicki's visiting a girlfriend."

"Oh, she must be out at a club. She isn't answering her cell. I was going to ask her to a movie. Why don't you come if you're not doing anything exciting."

I should have pressed the point about Vicki, but I was too curious. I wanted a close look at this intrepid, cautious, honest, thoughtful, spontaneous, mature, boyish figure of a man. He came roaring up in his Miata and off we went. We'd chatted a couple of times when he was waiting for one of my roommates, but he surprised me with how well he remembered, asking just the right questions. His driving was alarmingly fast but with an unerring efficiency that made my alarm feel silly. Besides he talked so steadily I forgot to notice his speed after a while.

"You do keep a harem, don't you?"

"What? It's convenient. You just call and there's bound to be someone."

"Aren't you afraid they'll get together and compare notes?"

He was parking but paused, turning to stare at me. "Do they talk about me?"

"Not with me," I said demurely.

After the movie, his place. Besides the famous mattress-couch with a fanciful Swedish light suspended over it, he had nice prints, an elaborate home theater system, two leather chairs and a coffee table made of driftwood and glass, a fancy little kitchen where I'll bet it had been a long since he'd had to make himself anything more taxing than coffee. He fixed martinis and we sat on the couch to the accompaniment of good jazz, soft, discrete. But instead of Allen the Hewer of Honest Intentions or the Boy with the Bounce in his Feet, I was treated to hip Allen, Allen the cold eye, viewing with quiet distaste this bleak crummy world in which we manipulate each other.

His voice grew lower, he leaned on his elbow, his lean eager face fashioned into a mask of cool world-weariness. Something hauntingly familiar. Then I located it. His voice had gradually picked up the rhythms of my speech; he had learned my language already. He was a smart boyo, I'll give him that. All the while his bright squirrel eyes were asking me, how about it? Do I please? I felt a sharp anger at him, the clever perfect student picking up clues to the professor's quirks. At the same time the flattery was potent, all that intelligence and charm bearing down, that this was the real Allen. I went there curious, kept my distance.

I pressed Vicki's friend's number on him, and he must have called because she came back the next morning looking a couple of years older and quiet for once. All she said was, "I'm seven kinds of stupid."

I was out Friday with a bunch of friends, but I found out the next morning that Cam wasn't back. Vicki crouched in her bed, her face spotted with ink from chewing a pen, the floor littered with balled up papers I could see were fragments of a note she would never mail.

Late Saturday afternoon, Cam arrived. They looked at each other, wary.

Vicki asked, "Why couldn't you come home? Couldn't you do that?

"I was finding something out. It doesn't matter now."

"I'd rather have found out for myself."

"I had to find out for me."

Vicki stared without speaking.

After a while Cam continued, "We'll have to be frank with each other."

Vickie snorted. "I have been frank."

Cam sighed. "Allen has been acting innocent about what could have upset you. He claimed nothing had changed."

Vickie stood and paced for a moment. "When I begged him to explain, he said it wasn't a mistake. Then he made a speech about how he is only half a man. The shadow of Janice hangs over him. Occasionally the shadow lifts, and then he can really see another person and care for her. These were just times when the shadow lifted. Then a lot about how he wants to break through and maybe I'm the one to help him." She sank into a chair, grimacing. "He looked so sad I fell into his arms and we hoisted the damned shadow again."

Cam rolled her eyes. "That's a fair approximation of the speech I got when I asked him what I meant to him."

"I thought you weren't interested in him that way."

"I wanted to be sure. I was surprised when you came home that day, because for a while things have been happening."

"Cam! You too."

"But he tried the same thing this morning and topped it off with a lecture on my defenses. You can never get anything worthwhile unless you take chances, he said, and open up emotionally."

"That something worthwhile is him? We sure repaired his ego."

They got madder and madder. First they decided he was sampling them to choose. Then they decided he didn't care which body was there, so long as it was warm and female. He had made each feel she was the one he was interested in, and that as soon as he was ready for a real relationship, it would be with her.

I excused myself, leaving them to their angry spiral. I heard them leaving, but paid no attention. I was seeing Allen. If he wanted to buy me supper, why not? I was curious what he'd say about recent events. I told him I'd pick him up instead of him coming for me.

The door was unlocked. I knocked once and walked in. The room was upside-down. Broken crockery on the floor. Torn papers. Books and magazines strewn about. His pillow ripped open and feathers stirring in the breeze of my movement. The draperies were pulled from their rods, those leather chairs overturned. Ketchup was rubbed into the mattress and the Swedish light pulled apart.

"No permanent damage," he said quietly. "Pillow easily replaced." He was sitting on the floor with a wet towel over his face.

"Your harem rebelled."

"It wasn't a harem," he said with irritation, then added smoothly, "To have a proper harem you need at least six or seven. Now I'll have to begin collecting from scratch." He waved me to one of the overturned chairs, letting the towel fall to his shoulders. "It takes two or three girls like that to make up one interesting woman, mature, like yourself. Women who know what they really want are rare ..."

"How long did you think you could keep on fooling them?"

"I suppose you know quite a bit? I can't understand how things got so congested. They didn't seem the jealous type ... I suppose we should start cleaning up."

"They outnumber and outweigh me. I don't think I can afford this supper." I started for the door.

"Let's do it another time." He put the towel back on his face.

I didn't answer. I had lost interest.

Vicki began to feel guilty about what they'd done and moved in with her friend from the office. We advertised for

a new roommate. The new one is more my age. Cam worries
me. She got a promotion and decided to buy a Prius. She is
doing the cooking regularly and gaining weight. She says
nothing real happened with Allen, but I have the feeling
now that as far as men go, nothing ever will.

The Shrine

Sonia drove the Mercedes alone to Ithaca. She had not expected Ron to visit her sick mother with her—her mother had endured two episodes of breast cancer already, meaning she had been seriously ill for the best part of the last four years. Now it had spread to her bone marrow. Not that her mother was ever less than serious and Ron had several important meetings.

Sonia made good time. She had an instinct for speed traps and only once was given a ticket in her whole adult life. It was a knack, knowing when she could speed without trouble. She thought of it was almost a metaphor for her life, knowing how to execute, know when to take chances and when to play it safe.

The Upper East Side to Ithaca took over four hours, everyone said, but she made it in three hours and thirty-five minutes. Her mother had been moved from the hospital to hospice the previous week. Was she really, finally going to die?

She followed the directions on her GPS. The hospice was unimpressive after the hospital, a former Victorian home. She parked, took a deep breath. Repaired her hair and makeup. She disliked seeing Frances if she were not well prepared, but how tough could it be if Frances was actually dying? Nonetheless, she fixed her face into a mask of concern and got out of the Mercedes. The heat struck her full force. It was only June 23rd, but her stilettoes sunk into the tar of the parking lot. In her head, Frances lectured her on how such high heels injured the back and who could remember how many inner organs? That typified the attitude with which Frances confronted the world. Never mind how you look, just be correct.

She was ushered into the private room by a tiny woman with coarse grey hair hanging down her back clasped with a barrette in the shape of a butterfly.

"Frannie! Your daughter's here to see you," she burbled.

Frannie? She was surprised her mother let the nurse or whatever she was use a nickname that Sonia herself never uttered. Frances looked ghastly. There was little color in her face and she had lost so much weight she looked papery, her small bones jutting almost through her translucent skin. The room did not look like a hospital room. Sonia was a little shocked. She expected tubes, machines bleeping or blinking, the usual when Frances was hospitalized. It was just a bedroom with one tube with a little button. The room was full of flowers, probably from her mother's old patients.

"What kind of medication are they giving you?" She bent and pressed her lips lightly to her mother's forehead.

"No medicine. Morphine. At the end, I'm becoming a drug addict." Her voice kept its husky dramatic quality. "I don't suppose at this last stage it could be considered a problem."

She was about to ask how her mother was, but stopped herself. A senseless question. She rephrased. "Are you comfortable?"

"They do what they can. They give me a matter of weeks."

"Weeks?"

"Four, maybe five if I'm lucky—if that's what you call luck . . . Where's your husband?"

"He's in a meeting. I came up alone."

"Deciding what new kind of financial scam to visit on us poor folks who don't run Wall Street."

Sonia took a deep breath. She would not rise to the bait. She was a clever trout, a rainbow trout, facing into the current, keeping safe by a big rock. Ron fly-fished sometimes. He found it restful. She would go along with a poetry book by some poet she considered possibly interesting or just her iPhone if they had reception. She would arrange herself on a shady bank in her Phillip Lim slacks—she had half a dozen as they were her favorites—and some more casual top. She would have a hat along in case shade was not available. She took care of her skin. Some women who had begun their twenties fully as beautiful as herself looked like leathery hags by now from their sun worship.

Her mother was talking about some local skirmish with developers she still tried to be involved in from her death-bed. Sonia nodded and murmured, staring at her mother, trying to find remnants of the beauty that had been Frances, that she herself had inherited. Not that Frances had ever had the sense to use what genes had given her. She barely wore lipstick. She wore loose pants, sloppy tops and those green smocks doctors affected. She had been twice married, her mother had, once to another medical student. That had produced her and her younger brother Carl, but her father had the brains to start a lucrative practice in plastic surgery that brought him to New York, while Frances dithered on with patients who often could not pay at all. The second marriage was to a local politico who left her eventually because her practice sopped up her time, leaving little for him, so he took up with one of his young admirers.

"Have you heard from Daddy?"

"George? Gorgeous George. Not in years. Why would I hear from him?"

"Just wondered. I had lunch with him last month. I did tell him you were having a relapse of cancer."

"I'm sure he was fascinated. So how's your health?"

"Healthy as a horse."

Frances held up a claw-like hand, the one not connected to tubes. "That's a silly phrase. Horses have many problems. Especially overbred ones. Do you remember my friend Martha, the vet?"

"Vaguely." A big homely woman. No wonder she administered to farm animals. Frances had met Martha when a horse kicked her, so Frances took care of her broken collarbone and arm. All Frances's friends had been dowdy wrecks, as she recalled. When her mother was home, one of those hapless females always seemed to be around talking politics, plotting some silly protest. How she'd resented them, taking her mother's attention, praising Frances for wasting her time on charity cases and lost causes, forever hanging around.

"You just missed Carl. He was here the last two days. He stayed in the house, as I hope you will."

"I have a reservation. Tomorrow I must be back." She was glad she had missed her brother. They had absolutely nothing in common. Carl didn't even have a relationship with their father, George. She had made sure to keep up hers. Her father had done a little work on her loosening throat, quietly, no charge. The money did not matter, of course. But she trusted his skill.

"What's Carl into these days?"

"He runs his organic dairy farm in Vermont, same as the last ten years."

Cows. Typical. He'd married one.

When Sonia escaped, she cancelled her reservation and drove straight back. It was a great relief to be on the road again. Frances hadn't even asked her about her new book, how it was doing, nothing. It had been published by a prestigious university press, Wesleyan, and received decent reviews. Of course she had as always sent Frances a copy. She had managed to keep up her reputation as a poet in spite of not teaching, except for an occasional brief stint. After all, she had no need to do the dreary work of teaching undergraduates who pretended to be writers while spewing their callow verbal vomit. It was bad enough to have come from a family of losers; she had no desire to associate with more of them. She had not squandered her advantages—good looks, intelligence, talent in a field with little money but some glamour—to marry well and keep that marriage alive. She had been faithful to Ron and only flirted with other men when there was some advantage to it. He had lapsed briefly but she had forgiven him. She was not stupid enough to let go, although she could probably manage a good settlement by now.

She had done well with their son and daughter. Liam was climbing in the same firm Ron worked for and Madison had married a lawyer with political ambitions. Madison was expecting. Though Madison lived in Denver, she and her daughter were in weekly communication. She would fly out there for the birth if she possibly could. She considered herself a much more effective mother than Frances. She had a closer and warmer relationship with both her children than Frances had ever tried to have with her. Frances had always been disapproving, from puberty on. Why are you dressing like that? Do you ever think about anything but boys? Who cares about cliques in high school? It's all adolescent nonsense: never understanding she was studying how to manage men and other women, how to walk into a room, how to impress without seeming to be trying, how to flirt subtly but effectively. How to use little endearing gestures. She and her mother had lived in different worlds, and she was glad for that. Her world was so much more comfortable, so much more interesting. Frances could have had such a better life if only she had tried.

Sonia slipped back into her routine, the appointments, the parties, the trips to the Hamptons, the redecorating of the living room, the conversations with Madison and her editor, the dinners with Ron, his colleagues and clients, with Liam and his new girlfriend Mia—who would not last long, she was sure. She called the hospice three times a week; she understood the importance of playing an expected part. Solicitation was required; she provided it. She polished her poems until they were hard as diamonds and sent them out to the correct magazines. She had her hair lightened a shade and shopped with her friend Marlena, who always knew the best boutiques. She and Ron often spent weekends with Liam at their near-beach house, but she preferred going back to the city with Ron during the week, even during heat waves. Men left alone in a hot place could get into trouble. Liam dropped Mia and took up with a Brazilian model for a couple of weeks. He went on a fishing trip with pals and the model disappeared from their lives.

The call she was expecting, had been awaiting for years, finally came the Wednesday after Labor Day. Frances had hung on far longer than her doctors had predicted. Typical. Ron accompanied her to the funeral, crowded with her mother's seedy patients, nurses from the hospital, her brother Carl, his fat wife Annie and their four children ranging from fourteen to three, whatsit and whosis and whatever. Carl and Fatty had certainly bred. The offspring were all tall for their age and rangy, freckled and tanned and apt to stare at her. Even at the funeral, they were all in jeans. Ron found her brother embarrassing and she tried to keep contact to a minimum. She was always gracious to people like him. Once he had been good-looking enough. In high school he had been far more popular than she ever could be, because he played basketball. But he was aging rapidly, bald on his crown, his skin roughened by sun and weather, his blue eyes (like her mother's, like her own) perpetually squinted. Cows and goats and sheep he lived with. Why had he bothered going to college? What does your brother do? He makes cheese. None of her friends knew she had a brother.

Liam had found an attractive redhead and was sitting with her, looking more in her direction than at the service. Sonia fixed her eyes on the pulpit and ran through her week's appointments: yoga Monday morning, call Madison at eleven, lunch with Marlena, then her own work until seven or so when Ron would come home. Tuesday, spinning class, then straight back to her desk until she had a facial at four and dinner with two other couples at some new Asian fusion restaurant the *Times* had written up.

The service was resolutely nondenominational, Unitarian Universalist, and interminable. At last they were freed and declined the invitation to go out for meal with Carl, Annie and a gaggle of old ladies who had been friends of Frances. The three of them got into the Lexus with a tremendous sense of having done their duty. Escaping at full speed back to reality enlivened them and they chatted happily.

It was actually Tuesday before she got back to her desk for real work. In her middle drawer were all the notes she had created over the years for that moment when her mother was no longer on the earth to refute her and she could begin a series of elegies in sonnet form. Begin creating the myth of the beloved, hard-working, self-sacrificing mother and the daughter who cherished, adored and now mourned her. She would have an entire section in her new book devoted to those poems. That would silence those who admired her craft but complained about "the icy heart of her poetry." She'd heart them with all her power. She could almost see the reviews. She would create a color range of grey to blue in her imagery. Compare her to chicory that grew wild in vacant lots. Her hair to milkweed fluff. A frail woman who devoted her life to others, dearly beloved by all but especially by her devoted first born, her daughter. Now Frances was entirely hers at last to do with what she wanted. No distractions, no duties that were so much more important than her children or husbands, no patients calling all hours of the night with their petty emergencies, no local politics, no campaigns, no demonstrations. Frances had become a perfect doll for her to play with.

Carl could challenge her, but he was not about to start reading poetry, even hers. None of her mother's elderly friends would be a problem. The myth was hers to shape and amplify. At its center, the grieving daughter whose love for her mother created a shrine of words. Turning on her computer, she smiled. Long ago she had planned how to write this sequence and now at last it could be done.

The Easy Arrangement

In my life, there have been a great many Mr. Wrongs. I married one of them and spent time and energy and emotion on dozens more. My feeling is that in love you are entitled to a great many mistakes so long as you aren't making the same one over and over. I have friends who always fall for the same man in various guises. One dear friend insists that she must have the right chemistry, a template in her brain that must match up for her to fall in love. That template ensures that the man will never be faithful but treat her like a recalcitrant dog.

I have managed, however, with persistence and gullibility to commit a great many different mistakes, a whole galaxy of flaming errors. One of them I'll call Oscar because that was not his name.

Oscar was an intriguing mixture of bad boy and respectable professional. He taught American Studies at Sarah Lawrence. He was very "political" as those of us who work for social change use the word, meaning in this particular case that he had the vocabulary of a revolutionary but wasn't one. He could sound quite the rebel, but he taught his classes and graded his papers on time, paid his taxes, was good to his parents and in truth an upstanding bourgeois son from an upper middle class family, raised in the suburbs of New Jersey off the Garden State Parkway.

His students liked him and he got on with his colleagues unless he chose not to. While I was living on the Upper West Side of Manhattan, I met him when he interviewed me for the *Village Voice* after my second book of short stories came out. He flirted with me and I flirted back, but I was married at the time so nothing more happened. A few years later after an acrimonious divorce, I moved to Boston where I found a temporary gig teaching fiction part time at U Mass Boston.

I teach many workshops for aspiring writers, read from my stories and give the odd lecture. I don't know if Oscar actually arranged for me to give a reading at Sarah Lawrence or if someone else on the faculty suggested my name, but certainly when I arrived, he took credit for the invitation. He chauffeured me about, was attentive and charming. He was quite deferential in soliciting my opinions. "If a man can be a feminist, then I'm proud to be one," he murmured. One of his colleagues was annoyed I had been invited instead of a respectable fiction writer adorned with establishment prizes. "Who are you to address our students?" he demanded over supper.

"Someone the students will actually relate to for a change instead of sneaking out or spending the whole time texting how bored they are." Oscar defended me with passion and wit. I was grateful and intrigued. We made love in his Brooklyn brownstone apartment. I didn't know what would come of this event—whether it was a one-timer or something more meaningful.

He began coming to visit me in Boston, staying in my Brookline apartment, soon bringing me whenever he appeared presents of books he thought I must read. They were always by men, usually academic radicals like Marcuse and Chomsky. As a writer, I always have at least ten books I am reading at any given time and a list the size of the OED to be read soon. Books to be blurbed come in the mail almost daily. I would rather have been given Godiva chocolates or a pretty scarf, but oh well. He would not have thought such presents sufficiently correct. Once we had been to bed a few times, his deference wore off. Quickly.

He was a man of great self-confidence, a trait that I, like many women, tended to find attractive, although after Oscar I was less wowed by assertiveness. He decided it was too hot in the city and borrowed a Cape Cod cabin from a colleague for four days in August, when we were both off work. He could not see why we should walk to town on the busy road.

"Look, you can see town right across that meadow. Why not go straight across? Save half a mile and avoid the cars."

I explained that as far as I could see, the area was partly wetlands. He saw no obstacle in that and led the way. At first the going was difficult but passable, picking our way through brush and jumping a creek. By the time we had penetrated well into the area and thrust halfway through an enormous patch of bull briar, it was too late to turn back. Two hours later, soaked and caked with mud to the thighs, lumpy with mosquito bites and as it turned out upon later examination, crawling with ticks, scratched to bleeding with briars, we emerged in town. People passing us averted their eyes. We fought the marsh and the marsh won. We bought our lunch—takeout because no place would have seated us— and went home via the road. After this, I picked our routes.

A particular bay was posted as off limits to shellfish- ing. Oscar announced this was nonsense and they just were trying to keep regular people from enjoying the clams. "Why should we need a license to reap the bounty of the sea? It should be free to everyone. They're making private property out of what should belong to us." He had grown up in New Jersey near the ocean and he knew. Who was I to argue? I grew up in Chicago, saw the ocean for the first time when I visited New York my senior year in college, ate my first shellfish and lobsters then and had only been a full-time Massachusetts resident for a year and a half. We waded in and dug clams. It was new to me and interesting. We were sick for two days.

That was the usual digestive trauma caused by eating polluted clams. Oscar insisted it must be the way I had cooked them, but after that, I ignored his statements about the natural world. Still, I was fascinated by him. He was physically strong—had played soccer in high school and college—quite a different type from the scientists and poets I had been involved with. He was energetic and opinionated, as am I, so our evenings tended to be lively. His mind was good and he was widely read in his field and also in mine. As a lover he lacked finesse but offered enthusiasm—at times a bit too much pounding but at least he was ready and able at a moment's notice. I liked to cook and he liked to eat. I don't do well with men who are finicky trenchermen or on weird diets. Like me, he was an adventurous diner.

Our relationship went forward sporadically but intensely. I lived in Brookline in a sublet; he lived in Brooklyn. He came to me oftener than I went to visit him, but we always managed a long weekend or most of a week every month. We went out to jazz clubs, watched a Red Sox game at Fenway, dined in the North End. He was very particular about when I could come down, but I understood that his schedule was heavy and crowded. I am not by nature possessive and I am busy and actually like to write. We always managed to find a time that worked for both of us. We both had busy lives so a part-time relationship worked well. I was open about my ex-husband's infidelities and how they had hurt me. He was sympathetic and described his pain when his wife left him. I thought of us both as injured by love but in recovery. We were well suited, I thought, for such a partial commitment that might well grow into full-time over time. I looked forward to seeing him but was too occupied to pine.

One problem I had with him was his desire to have sex outdoors. I am not an exhibitionist; I believe beds are built to be comfortable for purposes that do not only include sleep. However, I was more malleable in my early thirties than I have been since. We joined our bodies somewhat clumsily in blueberry patches on Cape Cod, in my car on a residential street, on a deserted (we hoped) stretch of Cranes Beach, and memorably for him—I was on top that time—in a patch of poison ivy in Franklin Park. I never knew when he would get that look on his face that indicated lust and say, "Come on. Let's do it." Sometimes I agreed; sometimes not. I was glad when the weather turned colder and even he did not want to have sex in a snow bank.

I found the relationship to be just what I needed. After being married for nine years, it was a great relief to have frequent male companionship and sex without having to do his laundry, cook his meals, worry about his health, listen to his insecurities and in general provide upkeep and free therapy. I was delighted to see him when we got together. I rarely missed him when we were apart, because I got back to work, did what I pleased with my evenings and weekends, saw friends and kicked back. He didn't get in the way of my friendships with mostly women friends, a gay couple and some male colleagues; my husband had been jealous of time spent with people that were not his friends or colleagues.

Oscar was divorced, as was I; in fact I knew and liked his ex-wife Caroline. They did not seem to be at odds. We went along for a year quite comfortably. Then I was offered a short residency at Brooklyn College. It paid very well for the time involved. I expected that he would be delighted. I was not anticipating moving in with him, for the college was providing housing. I would be teaching a workshop, giving a public reading and lecture and several seminars, so I wouldn't have much free time, but obviously we would see quite a bit of each other while I was staying so near him.

I called the day after everything was confirmed. "Great news. I have a month residence at Brooklyn College starting in two weeks. I'm a last minute fill-in. The guy they wanted had a heart attack."

"What? In Brooklyn?" He almost yelled.

Probably excited. "Yep. In two weeks I'll be on your turf for a month."

"Oh." A long silence.

"I don't expect to move in with you, don't worry. They have housing for me."

"In Brooklyn . . ." His voice was thick but not with joy. "Why didn't you talk to me about this first?"

"I'm not in the habit of asking your permission for gigs. This one pays well, and I sure can use the money. Look, if you're worried, I'm not about to lean on you for entertainment. I only left the city three years ago. I have plenty of friends I want to spend time with. I know my way around."

Again a long edgy silence. "We'll talk about this again."

I had already signed a letter of confirmation, arranged for an absence from my sublet and written my lecture. I was disappointed that he wasn't delighted I was coming for a month, but people often respond badly to change in a routine that has suited them. Once I was there, he would see how great it would be to spend relaxed days or nights together. If he feared I would be overly dependent, he'd soon realize that was no problem. I continued emailing friends and acquaintances I wanted to catch up with. I got tickets to the New York City Ballet and a play I wanted to catch.

I did not have time to see him until my third night in the city. He came to the apartment that had been provided for me in Green Point. I assumed we would go out to eat, but he brought some Thai takeout and a six-pack of Tsingtao. I didn't need great intuition to see that he was angry, although I had no clue why. "You shouldn't have come to New York and parked yourself here for a month," he said, grimacing. He put the takeout down hard on the table but stood, glaring at me.

"I don't need your approval to come to New York. I lived here for seven years before I ever met you."

"But you expect me to eat with you, sleep over, run around to flicks. You expect to call me any time and drop in."

"I assumed you'd want to spend time with me. But I'm here making a living." I reiterated what I'd said on the phone, that I was not dependent on him. "I like New York. And I thought you'd be pleased to have some unscheduled time together."

"Unscheduled? Unwanted, you idiot." He continued to stand, looming over me where I sat. I disliked that and rose to my feet.

I was getting annoyed myself. "What's with you?"

"Jennifer won't like it. She's going to be pissed off. You've put your foot in it this time. How can I keep her from finding out when you're staying here?"

"Who's Jennifer?" I tried to remember his mother's name. Daniele, I thought. Why would this Jennifer be annoyed? He didn't have children by his previous marriage, and his ex-wife's name was Caroline.

"Only my girlfriend . . . My fiancée."

"Your what?"

"We're getting married in June."

"But I've been in your apartment several times. She doesn't live there."

"She's based in L.A. for now but she stays with me when-ever she's in town or off. She's a flight attendant and gone half the time. I always put her things away before you come. But now you've blown it! You've really blown it!"

"You've been carrying on an affair with me for a year and you have a fiancée you're living with? And you never thought to tell me?"

"I didn't tell her either. Obviously! She's gone a lot. Do you think I'm stupid?"

I jumped to my feet, gesturing. "No. I am. You're a liar. You're as bad as my ex."

He turned red as a radish and raised his fist at me, taking two steps forward. He shouted, "It's all your fault for insisting on coming to New York! You've messed everything up! How am I going to keep her from finding out?"

"Simple. Get out and stay out. I hate men who lie!"

"Shut your face or I'll shut it for you," he said unoriginally but with feeling.

I was afraid for a moment, then picked up a chair, holding it between us. He looked like a crazy mad pit bull, one the size of a rhinoceros. "Get out. Get out now. I never want to see you again. If I see you, I'll cross the street." I tossed his takeout into the waste-basket, trying not to look as nervous as I felt. He was much stronger than me. I glanced around surreptitiously for something hard to defend myself with. I really thought he might punch me.

He stood glowering for several moments longer, his fists clenched. But he was a bright man, cautious of his reputation. At length, he took a step backward. Snarling, he grabbed his six-pack and left, slamming the door so hard every loose object in the room shimmied and rattled.

I took a deep breath and stood there, my hands shaking. I locked the door and threw the dead bolt and subsided onto the couch.

Finally I got to my feet, fished the Thai food out of the trash and sat down to eat it. After all, I was still hungry. I took some pleasure in the image of him packing up all of his fiancée's things every time before I arrived and scrubbing away the traces of my presence before she returned. I wonder how he explained the scent of Opium on the pillows.

I felt humiliated. I had been having an affair with a man who belonged to another woman, not with her knowledge but behind her back—some feminist!

Three weeks after I returned to my sublet in Brookline and a manuscript whose deadline was approaching like a big truck whose brakes had failed, Oscar called. His voice was calm. "I have to be in Boston the weekend after next for a conference at Harvard. How about it?"

"I could care less. I have no wish to see you next weekend or ever again."

"Don't be silly. We could have a good time."

"My idea of a good time is seeing you drown."

To my surprise, my refusal annoyed him. I don't think he had anticipated that argument would be our last contact. Perhaps he expected me to apologize, pack up and go back to Brookline where he could periodically appear. Or now that I was off his turf, everything could return to what had passed for normal.

Of course he got his revenge. He reviews my books negatively in various small publications, always with some sort of dig about my man-hating. But I don't even hate him. I feel tricked but lucky to have gotten out when I did. I had been an idiot, he was right. Since then, I do some detective work on any man I consider bedding. I don't intend to get fooled again. None of my friends believe I hadn't guessed something was fishy, but I really had been blind. It was all so convenient, a lover who could be fitted into my busy schedule and made few demands. Such convenience, I have learned, always comes with a price.

What the Arbor Said

Light bouncing off the lake freckled the ceiling over the bed where Laura lay. With the boys at camp—Nat a counselor now and Ethan one of the senior boys—she was stunned with idleness. In the city she had PTA at Buttonwood Prep School and fundraising for the local hospital. At the cottage, her days had always been frantic with swimming, boating, fishing, entertaining her sons' friends on visits, sometimes colleagues of Derek's. Not so often lately. Derek spoke of selling the cottage for something more upscale, perhaps on the coast. She hoped not. She had such fine memories of this place. The boys would not need her as they had, best to realize that. As if a wind that had been blowing hard against her had suddenly fallen silent, her ears roared with silence.

She shook herself alert, going out to weed the marigolds and zinnias she had bought in flats and put in along the flagstone walk that led from the cottage to the lake and the dock where their motorboat was tied up. Now at least she had time to garden. The first week, with Derek in the city and both boys at camp, she had felt lost here. Now a rich thick content filled her as she knelt, letting herself gradually drift into her past. Once she had lived passionately, lyrically. Her favorite scenes glowed like amber stones told one by one, like those worry beads she had seen men use in Turkey. Derek had been in Istanbul on for a conference and brought her and the boys along. She had met Derek in college. His room, yes, every inch of it was radiant with memories.

Their parents had both been opposed to their relationship, judging them too young for commitment. Even the crises of the school year and their first narrow rooms in a tenement where mice scurried through the paper-thin walls belonged to romance. The door slammed behind Derek and he rushed to lay his heavy head in her lap and spill his day, his anger and jangling will across her thighs till he had calmed himself. Derek was a lion among fools and he loved her till the ceiling went away and her eyes fell back in her head. So long ago.

She had finished college, although she had understood obliquely that he had not wanted her to. He smoldered with jealousy of the men she borrowed notes from, studied with, sat by in lectures, chatted with between classes. He could not imagine that each one of them did not desire her. She kept silent, flattered. It proved his deep love. By the time she took her last exam, her swollen belly arched against the writing desk. Nat was already growing inside her.

In midafternoon Conway Gates came to the arbor between the cottages and she went to fetch her mending. Every nice day he brought a book to the arbor, but if she joined him, he would lay it aside. Poor lonely widower six years older than she, Conway taught chemistry and physics in high school. He came out here because he liked to fish in the early mornings and perhaps more simply because coming here was how he spent his summers, in a cottage he had inherited from his parents when they passed. Conway's hair was grey and shaggy, rising to a cowlick. His face was gentle, sad-eyed, long-nosed and hopeful. His caramel-brown eyes with their long sandy lashes greeted her with open eagerness as she took her seat, sewing basket in her lap.

They exchanged books. Conway would describe all she had no time for, exhibits, plays, visiting poets, the fad for straw masks. They gossiped about neighbors here and people in their separate lives. At each summer's beginning, they needed a week to sketch in their worlds. Their winter paths never crossed and Conway understood without her having to spell it out that when Derek was up from Boston she had little time for him.

Laura enjoyed how clever he made her feel, electric with perception. Sometimes in the middle of discussing some book, television documentary or film, sometimes in mid-dissection of a local scandal, she caught sight of her arm with a shock to see herself so womanly, unconsciously expecting the body she had years before when talk had been a lively duel and dead men's winey ideas had fed her instead of her own cooking.

Conway lived in an area of galleries and coffee shops, and he liked having friends who lived with more risk than he did. He liked intellectual friendships with gay men, but then he liked to know men who were successful with women, too. He enjoyed teaching, especially bright young girls who needed encouragement in science. He gave much time to student activities and clubs, was a well-liked chaperon at dances. But in summer, it was good to escape the city before the close fabric of his life sagged. In a Hawaiian shirt and Bermuda shorts, he would walk barefoot along the lake shore whistling, proud his legs were still trim and firm. He relished the contemplative silence of fishing and he enjoyed talking through the sunny afternoons with Laura.

Laura had short dark brown hair and wistful grey eyes, colors of autumn he thought matched her sadness. All the years of childbearing, hostessing for her domineering husband, cooking and raising boys had left her still graceful, although a little thick in the hips. He felt guilty noticing, but he could not help being observant.

She was married to a balding opportunist, one of those types with one foot in the university, one in the business world and an eye on Washington—something boring to do with economics. Derek had been born with a machete in his mouth. Conway disliked being with the two of them together. Derek would pace around Laura examining her from the contemptuous corner of his eye. "Wear the blue silk with the belt and remember two doubles of dirty martinis for him before dinner and damn it, allow time for that and don't start rushing people to the table when they're chatting."

Most likely she'd married the first man to show her attention. That coarse transformation that turned his shy minnow girls into man-hungry pikes. He saw her coming toward him cradling a basket against her, and the sensuous dignity of her walk made him swallow.

So they sat in the sun and shade of the arbor while she quilted. At Buttonwood, some of the mothers were in a quilting group. "I was thinking, Conway. You never speak of your wife. Is it that fresh, still?"

He looked slapped. Finally he said, "If I don't speak of her, it's because I feel more honest keeping quiet."

She waited, bowed to her fine stitches.

"We were happy when we were first married. She was lovely but fearful, out of a broken home raised by her father only, deserted by a mother who drank. But somehow I failed her. I wasn't ambitious enough, perhaps. Somehow I became that father and she had to betray me as her mother did. Or so I see it now. She left and came back, she left and came back. The third time she returned, she thought she was with child. I was sure it wasn't mine. But it was cancer instead. They operated three times, chemo, radiation. It took two and a half years for her to die." He looked at her hands a long time. Then he said in a parched quiet voice, "It was all expensive."

She felt battered. It seemed to her he was bleeding from the mouth. She put her hands on his shoulders firmly, instinctively. "How terrible—"

He bit his lip. "It's old. It's worn out. That's the fault of talking about it, don't you see? It doesn't matter any longer. Only . . ." He pulled her onto his lap, quilt and all, and kissed her.

She lay in his arms quite shocked, surprised by the softness of his mouth, the smoothness of his cheek, the taste and smell not of cigarettes but of the peach he had eaten earlier. She lay in his arms and unthinkingly, as if she were biting into a slice of cake she had been offered, she kissed him back, felt his lips on her neck, timid nibbling like a horse nuzzling. She rubbed her mouth against the smoothness of his cheek.

A car passed on the gravel road. She came to and pulled from him. "I must start supper," she stuttered and ran for the house. She was stung with shock as if she had been slapped all over her body.

That evening she couldn't give herself time to think about it with Derek home for most of the weekend. Then in bed she couldn't sleep for remembering, pondering what had happened. Does he love me? Has he wanted to do that for a long time? Did I accidentally encourage him? Was it pure impulse? Could he conceivably have thought that's what I meant when I touched his shoulder to comfort him? It was so strange for Derek to lie there sleeping bedside her not knowing anything at all, not knowing another man had embraced her. He would be furious. She longed to wake him, to confide the afternoon. But an explosion would result if she did.

No, she must be very careful not to hurt Conway's feelings and not to alert Derek. She must set Conway at ease so that they could go on chatting. She went over the strange afternoon trying to find signs and premonitions.

Lying beside Derek, stark awake in the first dull light, she rounded out a nice speech about impulse and maturity and friendship and the truth of moments.

In spite of lack of sleep, Laura felt exalted in the morning. She made a breakfast of an omelet with herbs from her little garden, grating Parmesan into it and frying bacon crisp. She wished she had oranges to squeeze for fresh juice. Derek brought a sheaf of papers to the table, but he complimented her on the eggs. "You seem in a good mood this morning."

"I was thinking of baking a blueberry pie. They're fresh this time of year. I bet the farmer's market has some in town."

"I'm cutting back on sweets, remember?" He looked up from his papers, frowning, his broad forehead crinkled. Once again she thought how handsome he was, still, a large broad-shouldered man with a strong chin and direct commanding gaze from his eyes the dark blue of lapis lazuli.

"Of course. Sorry! I wasn't thinking. Maybe I'll bake cookies to send to the boys."

"Don't. Ethan needs to lose some weight, not pack it on. You might think about a diet yourself . . . Keep us company."

She could not stay away from the window facing Conway's cottage. She felt astonished when she saw him looking as he always did, padding along the shore barefoot, turning over his compost pile, bringing in a couple of logs for his fireplace. She went over her speech, adding and subtracting and standing aside to admire. She changed into a sundress and washed, then brushed her hair thoroughly, as she always meant to but always forgot.

In midafternoon, he came out to the arbor. She paused, suddenly unwilling. Derek was on his cell, arguing with someone. She felt a little guilty. Would Derek think her unfaithful, to have kissed another man? It had been so . . . accidental. She recalled her period of jealousy four years previously when she had suspected him of an affair with a graduate assistant. Finally she had accused him and he had laughed at her. "Do you imagine I'd throw away my university career for some fling with a student? Don't be absurd."

She would have preferred he answer that he loved her too much, but Derek was pragmatic to the core—a trait that she generally appreciated. It had enabled him to give her security and comfort and their sons attendance at excellent schools, tutoring, sports equipment, the latest gadgets they desired.

She was being ridiculous. She walked down to the arbor, feeling her face heat. He laid aside his book as if reluctantly and began telling her about it, a tome on some new theory of learning. In detail, he set out its argument. She sat staring at him, wondering if yesterday had been some kind of delusion on her part. She could not stay there. She excused herself and hurried to the safety of the cottage.

It had meant nothing to him. She flung herself from room to room. A bachelor for the last six years, did she imagine he had known no women? He had meant the kiss as an invitation that, when she fled, he had taken as a refusal and considered the matter closed. How dare he offer her that kind of invitation. Or even worse, perhaps he had kissed her to turn the conversation from his dead unfaithful wife. Or been merely curious. The kiss had satisfied that curiosity. He had not liked her response. He had instantly regretted.

When she saw him in the arbor the next afternoon reading calmly and drinking something from a tall glass, she turned from the window and flung herself on the bed. That weekend she kept away, replied to his distant greetings with brief nods, glanced his way only when she was sure he could not see her. She broke a wine glass and, while slicing tomatoes, cut a gash in her thumb. She kept making speeches at him that left her unsatisfied, humiliated.

Monday after Derek had returned to Boston University for a meeting and still she did not return to the arbor, she saw him walking toward the cottage. She felt a pulse of triumph and then panic. What had she done? Now he was rapping on the screen door. Slowly she walked through thick air to let him in.

She pretended to be busy about the kitchen while they spoke in short sentences of broken rhythm. He cleared his throat twice. Suddenly fed up, she learned against the refrigerator and glared at him. "Why did you come up here? To talk about that damned book?"

"Laura? I had to talk about something. You looked at me so coldly. You seemed angry."

"Why would I be angry?" She said, already calmer.

"Laura, what do you want of me?"

"It didn't mean anything to you."

"What could it mean? Of course it did. You're a lovely woman ..."

Leaning on the cold slick refrigerator door, she looked at him with a chilly clarity. She saw a soft-bellied creature she had turned on its back. She saw that she could do anything with him. If she insisted, he would make love to her, he would carry her off to his neat Mondrian bachelor apartment.

"Oh, Conway, I am sorry. Do go home. We've both been very silly. I'll see you tomorrow in the arbor." She shooed him out.

Derek returned Thursday evening, instructing her about a couple he had invited for the weekend. His meeting had gone well and he would be enjoying a sizable grant to do research on certain consumer trends among retiring baby boomers. At breakfast he said, "What's up, or I should say, down with old Gates? I thought he was going to fall over his own feet when I met him on the road." He rubbed his not yet shaven chin, not really interested but his attention briefly caught as he waited for his coffee to cool.

She met his eyes, saying flatly, "Oh, he kissed me in the arbor last week."

"What? Why on earth?" One eyebrow raised.

"He was telling me about his dead wife. I suppose he feels guilty or embarrassed."

"Poor old loser." Derek shook his head. Then he gave a dry pitying chuckle and tasted his coffee. "Don't be too hard on the old bastard. Must be tough, all that young pussy year after year and nothing doing, not a paw on them or you're done for."

He drank his coffee and took his rod and reel to the boat tied up at the dock. She stood at the window, frozen. He did not care. He couldn't manage even a flash of jealousy. He did not care. She twisted her tee-shirt in her hands, let it drop. But I love him, she moaned, I love him! And he has grown indifferent to me. I'm just a convenience. Maybe he thinks of turning me in on a new improved model.

Again she retreated to the bed, pushing her face into the pillow. She wanted to cry but no tears came. Oh, how she wanted to be nineteen again, twenty-one, twenty-three when he had loved her, when they had melted in each other's arms. Why couldn't she have that again? Why couldn't she?

She turned onto her back after a while and closed her eyes tight. His room under the eaves where he had to be careful not to bump his head, the first place, the first bed where they had been together. When she entered, to the right was a red chair. Red, the color of tomato soup, and the bed was to the left . . .

Fog

Barbs was sitting at the dining room table of their little house in Portland just finishing up a tutoring session with a boy who could not comprehend algebra. He was failing the class and his mother had been referred to Barbs. Before retiring the previous June, she had taught math for almost forty years. She was patiently explaining that x and y were not always the same numbers (how dense was he?) when Didi came in.

She heard the door open and then smelled the Ombre Rose perfume Didi wore morning or night. Barbs had stopped growing roses, she was so sick of the scent. She had given Didi three other perfumes, but Didi kept saying that this was her signature scent. Barbs had given up.

When the boy finally escaped, Barbs got to her feet, stretching. "How come you're home? The shop doesn't close for three hours."

"Oh, sweetheart . . ." For a moment Didi looked blank. It always scared Barbs when her partner got that vacant look on her face. It had been happening oftener lately. Much oftener.

"What happened?"

Didi stood a moment looking at her purse as if it held the answer.

"Do you not feel well?"

"Angela doesn't want me to work there anymore." Didi collapsed in an overstuffed chair as if deflated. She began combing her hair. She still kept it blond and curly. She tossed her head with that gesture that used to make Barbs want to kiss her.

"Why?"

Didi shrugged. She put on a beseeching smile. "I'm tired. Could you make me a nice cold martini?"

"It's only two o'clock. Why did she fire you?" Barbs took off her glasses and cleaned them on her tee-shirt before putting them into their case and the case into the pocket of her slacks.

"How do I know? Stop picking on me." Didi got up and escaped to the kitchen. Barbs could hear her rummaging in the refrigerator. "Didn't you have lunch?" She called.

"I think so . . ."

"Don't you remember if you ate lunch?"

Didi didn't answer. Barbs had a pretty good idea why Angela might have fired Didi. Lately she'd become increasingly forgetful. She'd come into a room and stand there wondering why. She lost her phone, her keys, even her partial denture with some regularity, leaving it on an end table, on the couch, once in an old ashtray left over from when friends smoked. She had fallen twice in the last week, tripping over shoes she had left on the floor, tripping over their dog Simeon, who fled yelping.

Barbs went out on the back deck and called the shop. Angela answered. Barbs came straight to the point and Angela explained. "She keeps making mistakes with money. She's looking straight at an American Express card and she dials Visa. She can't keep bills or coins straight. I'm losing money on her. I'm sorry, but I just can't carry her any longer . . . Don't you think perhaps she should see a specialist?"

"You think I haven't tried to get her to one?"

Barbs sat in an Adirondack chair on their deck staring out at the lawn and the phlox in bloom, white and pink and magenta, the picnic table, the bird house, all the artifacts and plants they had put into their yard together after they bought this little house. Simeon came wagging to put his head in her lap. He was a mix of black lab and probably boxer, a good-sized dog with black fur and a rectangular head and floppy lighter ears from some ancestor. The yard was full of the warm weather accoutrements of Didi and her years together. They had been a couple for eleven years, longer than her relationship with Andie the tennis pro had lasted. For two years after that affair had gone bust, she endured casual pickups and friends' attempts at matchmaking until she was sick of trying.

Then she met Didi who was volunteering for the same candidate she was working to elect. Barbs had been out since college, but Didi was straight and married—but not very. Her son and daughter were grown and raising their own children. She had caught her husband cheating on her twice and was deeply discouraged. She knew he was seeing someone. She began confiding in Barbs.

Didi had been cute, even at fifty-nine—a womanly figure, a flirtatious little giggle, a way of tossing her head and looking out from under her lashes. She had been a buyer for a department store chain before breeding and she still had a sense of style, although very feminine and rather flowery. When Barbs thought of that time, she saw Didi in her summer dresses, always beautifully tanned, always put together. But sad. She wanted to protect this woman who had been sorely used and was being cast aside. Even her occasional ditziness was charming. She was so different from the women Barbs had been involved with, someone who needed taking care of, someone she could make a home with. Didi was three years older than Barbs, while her tennis pro had been eleven years younger. An older woman was less likely to leave her. She was keen to be partnered for life. Didi needed her, and she was ready to be the steady foundation under her.

Seducing her had taken patience but then Didi had exploded into orgasm, something she had rarely experienced with her husband. She instantly proclaimed herself a lesbian and moved in with Barbs. Her husband had not contested the divorce; he seemed on the whole rather relieved to offload his wife. Her daughter Cordelia and husband Nick accepted them quickly, but the brother, Spencer, four years older, sulked. Resented. Always wanted Didi to visit without Barbs, which was no problem for Barbs, who found him a bore and darkly conservative.

Didi and Barbs. Barbs and Didi. They were a couple in their Portland neighborhood, in the lesbian community, in local and citywide organizations. They agitated for gay marriage. They supported liberal candidates. They worked to clean up their neighborhood and get stop signs and street lights where needed. They hiked in the great park across the river and once took a white rafting trip, but Didi fell in the river and was miserable. They had had a good life … until recently. And mostly. She had been disappointed, she admitted to herself only reluctantly, by Didi's silliness, her love of dreadful romance novels that were mostly heterosexual, her unwillingness to learn even elementary Spanish when they went to Mexico or French when they took a vacation in Paris. She still said gauche things that made Barbs wince. She filled their house with gewgaws, a brass Eiffel tower, pillows with doggies on them, a whole collection of china shepherdesses and sheep that filled a corner cabinet. Barbs's taste ran to the stark and simple. Her favorite artist was Brancusi. A love of mathematics, she felt, led her to the core of design. Barbs and Didi were a compromise from the first year. But the important thing, she had always felt, was that they were a couple, they were committed, neither of them would run off or give up on the other. They were in it for life. Nobody was perfect, but they managed okay. Loneliness was much worse. She was too old to go searching for impossible perfection.

She had managed to get Didi to their local doctor by making an appointment for her annual exam and the same for Didi right after hers. She had a private conversation with the doctor about Didi's forgetfulness and unsteadiness. The doctor asked Didi some questions, which she mostly evaded or couldn't remember. Afterwards the doctor called Barbs and strongly recommended a neurologist give Didi a real looking at. Didi objected. "There's nothing wrong with me. Nothing at all! You're just picking on me again. Nothing I do satisfies you any longer." She pouted for two days.

Barbs was angry with herself for not being able to insist on Didi getting checked out by a specialist. She was angry with herself for the way all the little gestures and giggles and silly jokes she had once found charming now grated on her so that she was constantly reining in her temper. Didi was dependent on her, something she had found pleasing, some-thing that had made her feel secure in the relationship. Now that dependence felt more like dead weight. Yet in spite of everything, she had loved Didi desperately and long. She still loved her, she was sure, but somehow it was lost in the cloud that seemed to surround her partner.

After Didi left the gas burner on the stove turned on and forgot it till the kitchen curtain caught fire, she finally got her to a neurologist. "The house might have burned down. I only caught it after the curtain was ablaze." Simeon had barked and barked, alerting her. She had torn down the curtain, thrown it into the sink and turned the water on full blast. But the accident so easily might have been a tragedy.

"I forgot for a minute. Everybody forgets sometimes."

But the fire scared Didi. She let herself be carted off to a neurologist at one of the large hospitals. Barbs cancelled her tutorials, but she was surprised that it took all day. At the end, the doctor called her aside. "My opinion is that she is in the early stages of Alzheimer's. We can give her medication that will slow it down some. I don't know what you want to tell her, but my advice is that it's a lot for her to handle. She seems too fragile for such a sentence. You know we have no cure yet."

She felt as if she carried a boulder in her belly. A huge doom squatted on both of them. She called Cordelia, who wept on hearing the news. "Are they sure?"

"The doctor seems pretty confidant in his diagnosis. I could get a second opinion ..."

"It's terribly sad. Poor mother. But I don't know what I can do from here. I'm up to my neck getting Christopher ready for college. Nick is on the road more and more since he was promoted and I'm stuck with everything for the house and the kids. And Alicia is a handful!"

Spencer was blunter. "You wanted her enough to break up her marriage. So you deal with her. She's your problem. I've got enough of my own."

She began to hold Didi oftener, to comfort her for the end Didi fortunately could not imagine. Even when she did not feel particularly loving, she made herself act out affection. She made sure Didi took the drug supposed to slow the progress of the disease. After a series of burnt disasters, she took over the cooking, although sometimes Didi would forget, start to bake cookies and leave off with a mess in the kitchen. She had to be watched. She turned on the bath water, wandered off till the bath overflowed, shorting out some wiring in the basement.

Barbs imagined that her life now was something like having a young child. She also found that acting out affection actually seemed to increase it, mixed with a large dose of pity. Gradually they stopped seeing their friends; it was too difficult. As the months slogged by, Didi began to forget who they were and sometimes made inappropriate comments like "Who is that fat woman? Do I know her? She should go on a diet."

Their social world collapsed to just the two of them until Barbs found an adult day care where she could bring Didi five mornings a week. Didi liked it. She made friends with other senile women and enjoyed the games. Barbs began having coffee with friends. Everybody told her how heroic she was. She knew better. Didi often forgot Barbs's name, although she remembered who Simeon was. In the evenings they watched TV, although Didi seldom followed plots, or Barbs read to her. Didi would sometimes sing songs she had learned as a child or heard on the radio as an adolescent or a young adult. Barbs, who hadn't sung in years since quitting the choir at her parents' church, began to sing with her. Didi remembered the words to dozens of songs. It felt almost normal when they sang together. Simeon liked it too, beating his heavy tail on the floor as if he were marking time.

Cordelia called once a week, every Sunday, got an update from Barbs and attempted to communicate with her mother. There was no communication with Spencer. She had written him that Didi had Alzheimer's but got no response. Perhaps he considered it contagious or a disease of lesbians.

She remembered when she had first been with Didi, the changes that still were visible in her lover's body from childbearing had fascinated her. She had never felt a desire to breed, but she was insatiably curious and asked Didi dozens of questions about pregnancy, giving birth and raising babies. Now, she thought, now I know. I have a child but she is growing backwards into babbling and then silence. But I made a commitment: partners for life. But she will leave me, not physically but mentally. And for the first time since she was sixteen, Barbs wept.

What and When
I Promised

Circa 1947

I was ten years old and visiting my grandma Hannah in the mixed poor Jewish and African American ghetto where she lived upstairs in a wooden tenement. Part of every year, *bobbelah* stayed with us in our little asbestos bungalow in Detroit and we shared a bed. But several times a year, we went to Cleveland, where most of my mama's family lived. I loved Cleveland. In Detroit I was a secret Jew, since religious observance annoyed my father. In Cleveland, I went to *shul* with Hannah. In Cleveland it was all right to speak Yiddish. In Cleveland my aunts and uncles hugged me and fussed over me. In Cleveland Hannah made a Pesach Seder. In Cleveland all my uncles told outrageous jokes at the table. Everybody laughed with their whole bodies. We had plenty to eat in Cleveland. Good food and houses with books and music, even when the apartments were small and crowded. I was absolutely sure my grandma loved me; I was only as sure about my cat Buttons. I was doubtful about my father, who did not think much of me, and my mother and I were often at each other in kitchen skirmishes.

The big war of my childhood had finished the summer before. A great crowd filled the Campus Martius in downtown Detroit and everybody was yelling, shooting off firecrackers, kissing, dancing. I thought it was great. In our neighborhood, we kids had a parade with our bikes round and round the block waving a couple of flags and some balloons, banging on drums and shaking noisemakers left over from some New Year's Eve.

Grandma was my only grandparent. Both my father's parents were dead and my maternal grandfather's head had been bashed in by the Pinkertons when he was organizing the bakery workers in Cleveland. I had nearly a dozen and a half aunts and uncles and gaggles of cousins, but only Hannah to tell me stories from the *shtetl* where she had grown up till her marriage, stories of wonderworking rabbis, of the golem and Lilith and *dybbuks* and Cossacks. She had been hungry often, she had often been afraid, but she had belonged, the daughter of a rabbi, and she had many girlfriends with whom she bathed and washed clothes at the river and gossiped and shared her dreams. I knew that since the war ended, she had been trying to get in touch with relatives and old friends back there in Lithuania.

Grandma's apartment was tiny and mostly we sat in the kitchen with her cat Blackie and sometimes one of her neighbors who went to the same *shul*, where she would take me and we would sit behind the *mechitza*. At that age, I did not mind the segregation because I was petted and made much of by the old ladies who had the same thick accent as my *bobbelah*. They told me how smart I was and what pretty black hair I had, worn in two braids down my back.

Hannah was short and stout with chestnut hair streaked with white. She wore it in a bun, but at night when we shared a bed she would let it down like Rapunzel. At *shul*, she hid it under a tight kerchief, for my grandfather had forbidden her to cut it off when they married. I wished I had long hair like hers, but my mother cut it every two months. My mother's hair was as black as mine but kept very short. She curled it from time to time. Mine was straight and there was a lot of it. My mother would complain when she washed it with tar soap (she didn't trust me to wash my own hair) and then rinsed it in cider vinegar that I had enough hair for a whole family of girls.

Hannah wore thick glasses. She had made money doing embroidery but now she had cataracts and she said, "My eyesight, it's going too fast. Soon I'll be blind like a stone."

In Hannah's kitchen, neighbors came and went while her cat supervised from a high shelf. Most were Jewish and some were Black. That did not surprise me, as we lived in a Detroit neighborhood Black or white by blocks. My parents were openly prejudiced, but I had never lived in an all-white world. My first boyfriend was Black. That lasted until my parents found out and I was beaten hard by the wooden yardstick they used on me.

My parents had driven off to see one of my father's younger brothers in Youngstown, Ohio, leaving me overnight with Hannah. That made me happy, as I was the oldest and, she insisted, the smartest of her grandchildren, instead of a disappointment to my father for being born a girl. Also the woman married to my father's brother was just anti-Semitic enough to make sly hints and drop little phrases like, "That woman at my yard sale, she was trying to Jew me down on the price of the crib." Her son would pick on me when we were out of sight of the grown-ups. No, I was delighted to stay in Cleveland.

We had bagels and lox for breakfast with thick slices of onion and cream cheese that didn't come in a Philadelphia package as it did at home. I had brought my best doll. Hannah was making a dress for her out of an old tablecloth that had disintegrated. She could no longer do fine embroidery, but she could still sew by hand or on her old treadle machine. Late in the morning she sent me down to get the mail from her box. Proudly I brandished the key. Our mail at home was generally left on the front steps. Unlocking a metal box felt special. At home, I had just gotten my own house key that I was expected to wear on a string around my neck when my mother needed to be out when I was due home from school. Keys were very adult, I felt. I was old enough to be left alone. Kids were more independent in those days. At twelve, I would be babysitting until two in the morning.

An electric bill, a postcard with palm trees from my uncle Danny in the merchant marine, a circular for a new drycleaners and a thick official-looking letter from a Jewish organization. I carried them all carefully upstairs, proud of my errand and myself for doing it so well. I hadn't dropped anything and my hands were clean. I even brought up the circulars.

Hannah was laying out plates for lunch, the plates with roses around the edges that I loved. To this day, when I am a so-called adult and in fact a senior citizen, as they say—*bobbelah* would just say, old lady—I am fussy about my dishes, my mug for coffee, which sheets I put on the bed. My husband thinks this is crazy. I say it's because I'm female. Or maybe I'm just fussy.

She had soup boiling on the old gas stove that always stank a bit. "It leaks a little—like me," she would say if I mentioned the smell. (I won't give you her accent; that would turn her into a caricature and I had no trouble understanding her, including the Yiddish.)

She had a little radio sitting on the shelf that Blackie preferred, and often it would be turned to classical music or else the news. But whenever I came into the kitchen, she would turn it off. "Who wouldn't rather listen to you than some stranger?" she'd say. "What a nice voice you got."

"At school the music teacher won't let me sing. She taps me on the head to shut up."

"What does she know? A nice low speaking voice is nice for a woman."

Everything about me could use improvement according to my mother, and was just perfect by Hannah.

I put the mail on the table. She riffled through it and pounced on the official-looking letter, tearing it open and squinting at it. "*Ketselah*, read it to me."

"Dear Mrs. Adler," I read. That was her name from her second marriage. "In regard to your query about the following persons," and there was a list of perhaps twelve names I sounded out slowly.

"Yes, yes," she said, "*Mach schnell, ketselah*. Who lives?"

"We regret to inform you that all the inhabitants of . . ." I could not pronounce the name as there were too many consonants and almost no vowels.

She spoke the name and stared at me.

"All the inhabitants were killed. There are no survivors we have been able to trace."

She made a noise like I had never before heard, a shriek that went on and on as she beat her chest and shook back and forth. "*Alles . . . alles . . .*"

I read on. They had been shot, the entire village, and left in a mass grave. Relatives were trying to raise money for a stone monument. I did not know what to do except to rise and hold her by the shoulders, standing behind her chair. I was afraid. I felt too young to deal with her grief. I felt helpless and shaken myself. I tried to imagine what it would be like if everybody I knew died, how I would feel.

When she stopped shaking she said, "Because they were Jews. That's all. Little babies, my niece Rivka, my neighbors who had only one cow and two hens, the *Rebbi* my father taught, what did they ever do to anybody? Just because they were Jews, made to dig a big grave and then shot and piled in."

When she was cried out, she just sat in her chair, shoulders stooped and grey in the face. Her grief scared me. I had cried when my previous cat Whiskers had died. I cried over a baby robin I tried to save. I cried when I got beaten up at school. But never had I seen anybody weep like Hannah. The soup had boiled over on the stove and I shut off the burner. The scorched smell filled the kitchen but she did not seem to notice.

Finally she said, "Soon they will be no more Yids. They will wipe us from the face of the earth. We will be done. Four thousand years, and no more."

I tried to think what I might say. "Grandma, I will always be a Jew. No matter what, I will remain a Jew so long as I live."

She looked up into my eyes. "Promise. Your mother has forgotten everything. She doesn't know who she is any longer. Your father has no religion."

"But I do. I promise."

"As long as you breathe."

"So long as I have breath in my body."

She nodded. "I need *Yahrzeit* candles. I got to find out the day of their death so I can light candles for them and say *Kaddish*."

"I can write a letter for you."

"Do it. There's paper in the drawer of the little table." She pointed. I fetched paper and pen and wrote the letter she wanted and addressed an envelope. She sealed it and kissed the envelope. "This is all I can do."

"Should I go mail it?"

"Go ask my nextdoorsikah if she got a stamp."

I knocked, got a stamp and came back. "Okay." She nodded wearily. "Go mail . . . Do you mean what you promise me?"

I did. And I have kept the promise ever since.

Little Sister, Cat and Mouse

I don't wonder you had trouble finding the house. This tract is laid out in narrowing circles like Dante's hell. But why should Helena send me an ambassador? Remember her? You might say I have a few souvenirs of that summer. Here, somewhere in the desk, unless the children . . . This snapshot. Oh, it's one of those bridges over the Seine. It's a poor picture of her. The sun was too bright. That was Barry in the middle and me, in my Left Bank costume—I was such a fool! Yes, that was me, I swear.

She told you I was her best friend? Dear God. Like a country mouse she turned up in my apartment in Chicago fifteen years ago. I was in my second year subbing in the public schools, hoping for something better. She was in her junior year at Roosevelt College downtown. Not that she was country. We came from the same West Side neighborhood of square frame houses with a tray of grass in front, old enough for the houses to be sagging, near enough to the factories to hear their whine in the quiet of the morning. But I had left there when my parents broke up.

The evening she came to my apartment, it was raining. She looked like a wet leaf, her blond hair dripping as she sneezed. She had failed some test. She shivered, plucking at her skirt. "What a mean, stupid system! Science is unfeminine!" I thought she was going to cry, but she turned her anger on a mural my boyfriend Zak had painted, and after she had insulted it, she relaxed and we had supper. Her insults never bothered me. For all my troubles, I had then a placid confidence that attracted and annoyed her, for she could not know any better than I how flimsy it was.

In high school her mother had dressed her in prissy jumpers and drab skirts and buttoned cardigans, as if time had stopped in that house a decade or more in the past. Sometimes in the high school library, we had met in brief passionate exchange of books and music. Then from my three years' height I'd begin to condescend, and she'd batter at me in fury.

That fall, I was trying to cry on Walt's shoulder about my relationship with Zak without getting involved with Walt. Try to understand why I didn't stop to look at this kid who cadged meals, jewelry, five dollars, old lecture notes, and finally men. I suppose I should have been alerted when she turned up Helena: she was Elsie on the West Side. When I gave a party, I told her to come and meet some people.

Halfway through the evening, when I looked around for Zak to make sure he was not starting a fight, I saw him on the floor beside her chair. She got up and walked off. Then turned just as abruptly and intersected him as he was starting towards me. Zak: let me say he was big-boned, with a hank of black hair falling in his eyes, powerful hands and body he used with conscious arrogance. He maintained a violent past and painted in bouts. For almost eighteen months I had been his trampoline, running to my friend Walt for comfort and advice in between bouts.

So I looked hard at Helena. Her hair was that blond with seascape tones of green algae and sand. Her eyes were blue and perhaps looked so dark because the lashes were daubed a sooty black that blurred, as if they cast a shadow. She believed her sharp chin spoiled her face and told me she had grown her hair to soften it. But that sharpness brought out a questing, plaintive childishness. Did the sirens too cry, save me! take me with you! make me happy!

A week later I tried to deliver a warning, for I knew how Zak gobbled little girls with big eyes for breakfast.

"You have a compulsion to patronize me!" She perched on my couch with her knees drawn up, as if warming herself in her long hair. "Your life is shoddy, so you think others are shoddy too. Cow!"

She flung down counters of words like rolls of dice—words used to mean whatever she chose: "kind" applied from clothes to mountains; "nice," a hard, almost spiteful moral judgment hurled down and if not instantly accepted, hugged back into a silence now large-eyed and accusing; judgments gratuitous, sharp as broken glass: "shoddy," "gross," "ratty."

Two months later she had become the ingénue of a local theater in a loft. Zak, who had always advertised his heavy drinking, actually began to drink, and the last I heard, he was making movies for the training of traffic cops.

Two years later I met her on the Boul'Mich, and as the tourists trouped past the café tables, they looked on her as a genuine sight of the Latin Quarter, and surely they had their money's worth. It was mid-July and hardly anybody around but Americans and a smattering of Third World students. I'd been using my summer vacation to sublet a tiny apartment in the 10th arrondissement on the cheap and try to figure out the next move in my life. I was sick of subbing, didn't feel I had any talent for teaching children, and had no idea what to do next. In my room the growing pile of letters from Walt gave out ultimatums. He was getting his doctorate in chemistry with an assistant professorship at Stanford waiting. Short sure letters from a big calm man, who dominated me like a sandbag when I was with him. So I had posted myself at this crossroads waiting for the chance or man or decision to strike me, a long way from Chicago and hopeful that surely something more must be prepared to happen.

Helena's parents had sent her on a student trip as a graduation present, but she'd quarreled with the group. The hotels her group had booked she pronounced sordid. She began sleeping on a park bench, rising at six and washing at the spout, combing out her yellowgreen hair, then climbing over the iron gate before the keeper came at seven to unlock the park and threaten stragglers with a night in jail. She kept her clothes with me. She would wash her hair in the basin, leaving the trap clogged, lie on my bed and, folding her arms, denounce the way I kept house or fell in love. "You lack style," she complained. "Of course you'll marry your chemist. You'll have herds of fat babies and let them climb the furniture and you'll explain *everything*!"

After she found a room she would drop in at supper, to stand on one leg beside the table. She would talk rapturously of the chicken she had eaten a week before or the *biftek* of last night. She ate whatever I gave her, but if it were only spaghetti or eggs, her eyes left me in her debt. Whenever I fed her I felt as if I were acting a ritual, at once big-lapped mama and mean pinching stepmother.

That week my friend Jay turned up, with his deep baying voice of a good hound and his redbrown mane and glasses sliding down his nose. His affection came down on me with a hearty clatter. I remember him saying goodbye in Chicago, buttoning and unbuttoning his coat nine times before he summoned the spirit to lift me off my feet for a brotherly kiss, knocking our foreheads together. I'd known him since I was a freshman and we were lab partners in Zoology.

He came from his first meeting with her like a stung Saint Bernard. First he appealed to me to confirm that she had not looked at him in the café, would never look at him, was with that asshole in shades. Then he urged me to promise that tomorrow would be different. How did she live, poor thing? Something bad could happen to her. We did not eat till ten, because maybe she would drop by. Then he dragged me from block to block, from café to bar looking for her till we were barking at each other.

By the next night it was "Talk to her. All afternoon and she wouldn't say one word to me. She's the prettiest girl I've ever seen."

"The worst thing I could do is talk for you." But the situation weighed on my matchmaker's conscience. Besides, just once I wanted Jay to win a prize. He was much kinder and gentler than her usual pick-ups. He would be good to and for her. I told him to move some gear into my place and hang around looking intimate. The first time she really looked at him was when she saw him sprawled on my bed, while I stirred a pot and told her, sorry, this was supper for two.

Next day at the café, Jay draped his arm around my chair as we talked of going south for a week. I felt so clever as her plaintive glance coaxed at him and she dug her sharp elbows into the table and leaned forward. Oh, I know. To exploit her greed for anything that was mine was easier than to understand it. I only want you to see how easy it was to manipulate her, the quick solution to everybody's woes. They talked about kindness. She told him he was kind.

That weekend they left for the mountains of Provence, and I was treated like a sore toe. I felt the cost to my public pride small compared to my regained freedom. Then I squandered that August with a young French lawyer and his family in Brittany. There I tried to persuade myself that fulfilling his (and his mother's and his cousins' and his aunts') notions of wifehood would make me happy.

I got back to Paris in September just two days before my flight to find a scrawl from Jay, an address and a three times underlined, get in touch *immediately*. Apprehensive I sat on the Metro watching the Dubonnet signs flash past. I'd helped him put himself in the way of getting hurt, making him just interesting enough for her to pick up and drop. Still I was unprepared for his misery. He paced the hotel room, wiping his palms on crumpled pants, clawing at his stubble. They had spent the first few nights camping out, sleeping under a blanket wherever they could. Finally in a little hill town, they found a room. When they had to give that up because it was rented the last two weeks of August, they moved to a youth hostel in Fréjus down on the beach. They were both reluctant to talk about sex. Helena would have considered it vulgar to bring up and Jay was inexperienced and assumed she took the pill. It turned out she thought she couldn't get pregnant right after her period. She was wrong.

In Paris, she disappeared. Then she emailed him from Chicago that was she pregnant. He asked her to marry him. She refused. He could not get a flight out and his reservations were not till the end of the month. He had written, emailed, called repeatedly. Whoever answered in Chicago always hung up. So he paced his room clawing his scalp and bumping into me. I promised I would see her.

Arriving in New York with eighteen dollars, I wrote Walt a shamefaced email asking for a loan and took my luggage to a friend's apartment. I figured six days for a check to come, but by the fourth day, I was meeting the mailman. By the seventh, I thought silence an answer. I got a temporary job and called a friend in Chicago. The eleventh day a note came from Walt with the fare to Chicago and a ticket from there to San Francisco, to him, on the 20th.

I called from the station. Her mother answered. Helena would not come to the phone, but she had her mother tell me I could visit. On the bus I felt sick: headache, nausea. I kept imagining myself getting off and taking a bus right back to the airport. I had not been able to eat, and it occurred to me I was going through a mock pregnancy.

Kids passed in groups on their way to school, the backpacks, the clothes, the kids themselves looking very new. I saw the house, a wooden bungalow with every bit of ground sprouting a trimmed shrub circled by bricks, neat bathmats of lawn where I had often passed Helena's bald little father kneeling prayerfully with a trowel. Now on the front porch she was sitting beside her mother on an old porch swing.

I wanted to run. Her mother sat painfully straight with her hands locked like rigor mortis in the lap of her wash-worn tunic and baggy pants. Her eyes, blue like Helena's, had tight lines scored around them as if it had been a long time since she had seen anything she liked. Beside her with a jailed look, Helena wore a cotton dress that buttoned up the front. Her face looked childish without makeup as if her mother had scrubbed off her adolescence. I opened the gate and came up the walk lined with pink petunias as her mother rose.

"I understand you knew Elsie at school? You were with her this summer? And you know that man?" She made plain she understood the situation and it was no more than she had expected from allowing a young girl to run around. But Elsie had set her heart on going in spite of the cost—I could see they weren't wealthy, couldn't I?—and Elsie's father had given in to her with no more thought about what would happen than you could expect from a man. She was one of those women who talked to you woman-to-woman without liking you any better for belonging to their sex but to whom men are children, and children animals to be disposed of for their own good. Helena stared at the street, swinging idly. I was sweltering, aware suddenly of how much weight I had put on eating the cuisine of my French lawyer's family.

Finally Helena said, "Leave us alone, Mama. She and I want to talk. You can tie me to the railing to make sure I don't get away."

Sniffing, her mother slammed into the house. I sat

immediately. "Look, believe me, I'm sorry. Do you want to marry him?"

Her eyes turned so dark with anger she looked herself again. "*I* should marry *him*? He wasn't good enough for you."

"Look, if your mother won't help you, and I guess she won't, I think I can get the money for an abortion from Walt."

"And let me bleed to death or end up sterile! Mother warned me about abortions."

Talking to her was like sticking my fingers into a fan. She went on at me and all the while her mother was noisily vacuuming just inside. "You tricked me! I never would have slept with him, but you pretended he was yours. You made a fool of me. Did you go to bed with any of them? You're a fake!"

I was reduced to asserting my sluttiness. "Look, since Jay wanted you and not me, doesn't that put you one up on me somehow?"

"He isn't a man. He's a fool, an awkward bumbling child. Why should I want him? How could he be so stupid and get me into this mess?"

We got no further that day.

The next day her anger had muted to scorn and she would talk about the baby. Though with her slender body, all arms and legs, she looked less gravid in a general way than I did, both she and her mother spoke as if the baby were already in its crib. They convinced me she meant to have the baby, and that if Jay tried to see her, her mother would call the police.

Why did I keep going back? I couldn't let that police matron of a mother get her claws in another baby. I had started the mess by using Helena's peculiar regard for me, that backhanded possessiveness. And I was afraid, for her and for me. My last day I asked her to meet me for lunch. I still hoped I might talk her into taking the situation into her own hands. "Mama won't let me leave the house."

"But you're twenty-two—"

"Will you support me and my baby? Oh, you just want me to die!"

Since I was going to the airport, I brought my suitcase along. Her mother did most of the talking, listing grievances stretching from the hard life as oldest kid in a big family to her husband's worthlessness and her daughter's disregard. "I wanted her to be a school teacher, to rise in the world. But she didn't take her certificate. She studied playacting and she lied to me while we were paying for her useless degree."

After I called a cab, Helena came out on the porch to wait with me. I think my suitcase infuriated her. "Will you sleep with Walt? Oh, I hope you get pregnant too. What will I do with it?" She fixed her fingers into the flesh of my arm. "It's your fault, and I'll hate you as long as I live! I'm ugly now, because of you, you!"

A flash of conviction shocked me. I heard myself say, "Helena, I'll take the baby. I promise, I'll take it from you and raise it as my own."

"You're lying again." She still clung to my arm when the cab pulled up, and I was afraid she would not let me off the porch. As I drove away, I could see through the back window Helena standing beside her mother, a thin and angry prisoner. The print of her fingers and thumb stayed on my arm almost until the plane took off.

I sat on that plane in a frightened stupor, trying to make sense of things. I could not go all the way to California only to tell Walt I had not decided. I could not think. I felt trapped, squashed. As soon as I saw Walt at the airport, I began to run, and when he put his arms around me, I cried myself weak. I thought telling him the story might bother him, but he was very kind.

A month later we married, and I was pregnant myself when we flew to Chicago for Helena's delivery. Her mother wired me, but it was too late. Helena signed the baby away unseen. Sitting in that narrow house, she had a strange taut power and even her mother seemed wary of her. The rest of my pregnancy felt anticlimactic.

I wish her well. I owe her my marriage, in a way. Tell her I'm happy, and I hope she is. We have a boy, Alec, in high school and a girl, Paige, in middle school now, besides my baby, Abigail—she'll be waking soon. Walt's an associate professor and we do all right. By the way, he'll be home at five, so I need to pick up and start supper soon.

No, you don't understand. I can't see her. I'm not afraid of a scene, after this long. It's only that I have nothing to say, not even to myself. Isn't it funny? I was always mothering Helena. How could I have thought she was the weaker of us two?

I Wasn't Losing My Mind

My mother married for the first time when she was seventeen to escape a job as chambermaid in a hotel catering to traveling salesmen. She had been forced to quit school halfway through the tenth grade to bring in money to her poverty-stricken family with too many children to feed. The marriage was a disaster. She was more miserable in that marriage than as a chambermaid being sexually harassed by male travelers. She was able to get the marriage annulled, she told me, because it was never consummated.

Her next marriage was to a smalltime businessman with whom she had a son. That marriage lasted well over a decade. During the depression, she ran a boardinghouse to help out. There she met my father and eloped with him.

Whatever chemistry they had at first, and it must have been strong, by the time I was born it was gone. It was the marriage of the dog and cat. They could agree on almost nothing. Since he was the breadwinner, he had the power, but she was a great sulker. Although he did pretty much as he pleased—he bought a new car every two years while there was no money for her or me to go to a dentist—she had her own ways of making his life torturous.

My mother and I were much closer than I ever was to my father, who never got over the disappointment of having a daughter and not a son of his own genes. After all, she had produced a boy for her second husband. My brother came to live with us, and my father preferred him, although he was often harsh with him during his adolescence. I was even more rebellious. Both my brother and I left home as soon as we could.

She had few nice things, but one of them was a jade necklace my father had given her when they eloped. It had an oblong pendant intricately cut and hung on a fine gold chain with smaller globes of green jade set into the links— surprisingly delicate. I seldom saw her wear it. I think she felt few of her clothes were good enough to set it off. But frequently she would take it out, show it to me and hold it, finger it, admire it.

In a nostalgic mood, she would call me into her bed-room. She would drag from the closet a small pink piece of furniture about two and a half feet high with little drawers. It was small enough to be something made for a child. She kept it as far back in the closet as she could where it was hidden by my father's and her own hanging clothes. In its drawers were scraps of velvet, satin and silk, pieces of flow-ered cotton and rayon. They were not for quilting or patch-ing but rather as visible mementoes of her earlier life when she still could entertain hope.

She fingered a scrap of orange silk, worn almost trans-lucent. "I wore this gown to a party. It was for St. Patrick's Day and they all yelled at me for wearing orange. How did I know about their saints?"

She tossed her head, calling up the ghost of long spent flirtations. "But he asked me to marry him anyhow."

"Why did you turn him down?"

"He drank too much . . . Like your father."

She pulled out a bit of brown lace backed with green shiny satin. "This was one of Rose's costumes in George White's Scandals."

My aunts Rose and Evelyn had both danced in Ziegfeld Follies, other shows and revues, and Rose performed in the movies. My Halloween costumes were glamorous hand-me-downs from Rose's acts.

"Do you remember when I used to wear this?" A bit of turquoise cotton with white and yellow daisies. I remembered. She had still been beautiful then, her face like a flower: before her only pleasure was eating, especially cake and cookies and pies she baked.

But the session always ended with the jade necklace. She would take it from her jewelry box in which it was the only real piece, clasp it around her neck and finger it, her eyes going blank and blind as she revisited a more promising past than anything the present offered. She would rise abruptly, order me to shove the miniature chest of drawers into the back of the closet. Then as she returned the necklace to its place, she always said, "Someday this will be yours."

The last time we spoke on the phone, she reminded me that I was to have it. After they moved to Florida against my mother's wishes, we spoke every Monday when my father went out to play bridge at the senior center. She seemed afraid that my brother's fourth wife would take the necklace. As she was not ill, I couldn't understand why she brought that up. But then she had demanded we drive down the previous winter because she had something important to give me that could not be brought back on a plane. Again, when my father was out of the house, she collected dollar bills from every conceivable hiding place.

She pulled three dollars from behind a picture frame, dollars from her shoes, dollar bills under the lining of drawers, dollars rolled up in nylon stockings (she never wore tights), tucked into cookbooks and novels. She stood on a stool to reach dollars she had hidden on a high kitchen shelf (where all the whole grain and health foods I had sent her to control her blood pressure were stowed collecting dust), dollars hidden in a box of sweaters she would never wear in Florida. That night we counted slightly over $1,200 in single dollar bills she had saved from grocery shopping and hidden away from my father. That was what she felt that we needed a whole car to carry back to Massachusetts.

A few days after our last Monday phone call, she suffered a stroke. She lay on the floor while my father picked up all the pieces of a fluorescent bulb she had broken. Finally he called the rescue squad. My husband Ira and I flew down on standby the first night of Chanukah, but my father took her off life support while we were in the air. When we landed, she was already dead. She was perhaps eighty-seven. I never knew her real age as she had no birth certificate and made a habit of lying about her age, since she was considerably older than my father. She had had me when she was in her forties, about the age I was when she died.

While we were gone to Florida, I let my assistant Jean stay in our house, since she was going through an acrimonious divorce and seemed afraid of her soon-to-be-ex-husband. Earlier that year, Jean had complained of pains and gone to her gynecologist, who told her nothing was wrong with her except nerves. From her symptoms I did not believe he was correct. I suspect she had an ectopic pregnancy. I made an appointment with her at a women's clinic in Boston. Her pains got worse. When she arrived and was examined, they discovered that her situation was critical and the tube was about to burst. They rushed her into an operating room and saved her life. I had always treated Jean as if she were family. At my wedding, she was a member of the party. She was small, like me, but with light silver-grey eyes and a cowl of very short blond hair, a little pug nose, a laugh that always sounded as if it were forced out. Every workday, we had lunch together and gossiped and chatted. I was glad to have Jean in the house to keep the heat on and the pipes from freezing, to feed the cats, to collect the mail while I was in Florida.

My brother and his wife were already there when Ira and I arrived. I asked my father what we should do with her things.

"Throw them out. Get rid of them."

"You don't mind if we take some things?"

"Why would you want that stuff? Just get rid of it all."

Along with my brother's wife, I went through her things quickly. What I took were photographs, my own books signed to her—my father had never read any of them—some shawls I had given her wrapped in plastic and obviously never worn, the rings cut off her fingers by the undertaker and that jade necklace. She had so little to leave me and I knew how she had cherished that necklace, proof my father had once cared for her. (When I was thirteen, she made a fuss about wanting a present from him for her birthday. He bought her a kitchen garbage can.)

I carried it into the living room, where he was watching a football game. "Do you mind if I take this? I know you gave it to her as an engagement present."

"What?" He scowled at it before returning his gaze to the screen. "Never saw it before in my life." He banged his beer can on the arm of his easy chair for emphasis.

A year and a half after my mother's death, I was invited to a party on the Saturday night of Labor Day weekend and decided it would go perfectly with a linen tank dress in a color the store called celery. I always kept the jade necklace in my jewelry box in a little padded drawer by itself, a place of honor as my mother had always stowed it. I opened the drawer. It was empty. I felt true fear. How could I have misplaced or lost it? How? Certainly since my mother's death, I seemed to have been permanently scatterbrained, absentminded. I had lost more items in the intervening year and a half than I had lost in my entire life beforehand. But the jade necklace? I tried to remember the last time I had worn it, perhaps seven weeks before. But I was sure I had seen it more recently than that. But could I trust my memory? I had misplaced so many things recently.

I took everything out of the jewelry box. I crawled all over the bedroom floor. A flashlight revealed nothing but dust bunnies under the bed and in the bottom of the closet. I suffered with a stomachache all day. I must have looked in that drawer six more times, somehow expecting it to appear where it always was stored. Obviously I had done something stupid with it. Ever since my mother died, I had been misplacing things. I saw it as a metaphor, that since I had lost her, I kept losing other things, especially clothing and jewelry.

Monday afternoon of Labor Day, the phone rang. It was from Jean's roommate, Roxanne. Jean had been working for me for seven years at that point and had moved twice since her divorce. She had moved in with Roxanne the year before and told me what a pill she was, but Jean liked the apartment. She said Roxanne was a cow and jealous of her. On the phone Roxanne sounded very nervous,

"I don't know if I should tell you this. I really don't know . . ." Her voice kept rising into almost hysteria.

"Tell me what?"

"Jean has been stealing from you. At least for a couple of years. At first it was things she said you gave her. A sweater, a couple of blouses, a skirt, earrings, that kind of thing . . ."

"Stealing?" I couldn't imagine it. Jean had warned me that Roxanne was jealous of her.

"Food. A steak from the freezer. A bottle of wine. But lately she's been bringing home stuff I know you wouldn't give her. Fancy stuff. A gold Jewish star. A watch. A silver bracelet with turquoise set in it. A cashmere cardigan—"

"A jade necklace!"

"Yeah. Did you give it to her?"

"No! Never. It's the one thing my mother could leave me."

"Please don't call the police. I don't want to get into

trouble. Maybe I should've let you know sooner . . . It's making me nervous, all this stolen stuff in the apartment."

I was silent for a moment. My instinct was to handle it myself. "Is she there?"

"No. She's with her new boyfriend. She picked him up in a bar two weeks ago and she's been spending every night with him."

"Give me directions. I'm coming over to get my stuff."

Now she was silent. "I don't want to get in any trouble."

"You won't. She can hardly complain that I stole my own things back. But if I were you, I'd kick her out or move before she does something worse." I could not remember being angrier in years, maybe since my father had turned off my mother's life support while we were flying down to Florida. Betrayal—that's what I felt. I felt angry and I felt betrayed.

Ira remembered strange things that had puzzled him at the time. Once he had walked into her office downstairs and saw bags of groceries. Why would she bring them to work? Another time when I was out of town, he saw her wearing a dark gold sweater and said, "I gave my wife one like that for her birthday."

She answered, "I liked it so much, I bought one too."

Several times when I was traveling, she had acted seductively but he had just ignored it. He didn't say anything because he wasn't sure and he didn't want to get her into trouble if he was wrong.

Ira drove and we found the house without difficulty. The apartment was accessed by a back stairway in a white clapboard house. The second floor had two apartments. The one Roxanne and Jean shared was in the back of the house, a living room with a corner kitchenette, two bedrooms. Roxanne greeted us nervously. "I don't know what she'll do." She was a tall boxy woman with a long bark brown ponytail wearing old jeans and a new Red Sox tee-shirt.

"She's the thief." Nothing was going to stop me now. "Which is her room?" I waved the bags I had brought.

Roxanne pointed. Then she shut herself up in the bathroom. I had paid so little attention to her, I doubt if I would have recognized her in the street. I was focused. I was on a mission.

Jean's bedroom was a mess, the bed sort-of made, cosmetics scattered all over her vanity, along with a bottle of Femme perfume I recognized and plopped into the first shopping bag. I began going through her drawers. I didn't care if she arrived or not. I didn't care if what I was doing was legal or not. I found the necklace quickly and in fear that somehow it would disappear, I put it on. I found other jewelry, including a gold Mogen David on a chain that my husband had given me. Jean was not Jewish. I also found the clothes, the watch, the jewelry, the other items I thought I had lost. I collected them all—sweaters, blouses, scarves, a patterned half-slip, the silver and turquoise bracelet a friend had given me in Arizona. A half-open bottle of wine I was sure was stolen too was on her dresser, but that I left. I had the urge to pour it on her bed but resisted. I took nothing that I did not know for sure was mine.

I felt hurt that Jean would do this to me but also relieved that I had not lost my mind, had not become dangerously careless or absentminded. Roxanne told me as she ushered us out, almost pushing us through the door, that she did not expect Jean to return but thought she would go straight to work with me the next morning.

When she arrived Tuesday morning, I was wearing the jade necklace. I confronted her. I had placed all the items I had recovered from her bedroom in a pile on the table.

She kept not looking at me and I kept saying, "Look at me! What am I wearing?"

She kept saying her mother had given her the jade necklace and her boyfriend had given her the Mogen David. She wept.

I had a great desire to hit her, but I kept myself under tight control. I spoke quietly throughout, an edge on my voice but speaking softly so as not about to allow the scene to degenerate into a shouting match. I just wanted her out of my life. I wanted never to see her again, never again to have anything to do with her.

"You're fired," I said. "Now get out."

"Are you going to call the police?" She had stopped crying and was squinting at me.

"Not if you get the hell out and never bother me again."

She looked once more at the pile as if hoping to reclaim something from it. Then she picked up her purse and started out. She turned. "Does that mean you won't give me a letter of recommendation?"

I never heard from Jean again, but I did hear about her. I didn't ask, but people who knew the story told me tales. Nothing good. Cocaine and man trouble. I will never understand how I had failed to suspect her but, as I said, she had been with me for seven years and I considered her almost family: but family can turn on you as easily as a stranger. Now I remembered signs, walking in on her looking into the refrigerator, her constant sniffling that had begun after her divorce—but I knew little about cocaine. How every time I came back from a trip, I would miss something. I felt like a fool, but mostly I felt relief. I still have my mother's jade necklace, and every time I touch it and every time I put it on, I think of Mother and I still miss her. I don't think missing a mother ever stops.

How to Seduce a Feminist (or Not)

Mid '70s

Sheila had known Gill on and off for a decade in flashes since she was based in Chicago and he in Los Angeles. They had both been both active in the anti-war movement and met occasionally in mass demonstrations or events where one or the other was giving a speech. She had gone on into women's liberation and a teaching job at a small liberal arts college, he to the media where he was a frequent commentator on political issues. He was good-looking and photographed well, came across on TV as roughly charming with a warm grin.

Gill wrote that he was coming east for a conference in Chicago in July, suggesting he visit her. Could he stay since the budget for hotels was adequate only for a Red Roof Inn out in the far suburbs? She said, sure. She had a floor-through in an old brownstone on the near north side—not yet upscale at that time—and a spare room. Friends not infrequently came through town and stayed. She generally made a pot of stew or soup that lasted her several days, but cooking for the occasional guest gave her an opportunity to try out something from the several cookbooks she had purchased for her kitchen.

Gill arrived at O'Hare and was picked up by someone

from the conference and dropped off at her apartment around seven. Sheila had prepared a chicken dish that could sit in the oven turned down to 175. He said he had eaten on the plane but chowed down as if it had been a week since he'd tasted food. She was pleased; if she went to the trouble of cooking, she wanted her food appreciated. "God, this is really good," he said several times. "Perfectly cooked, well spiced." During supper he regaled her with stories of his recent appearances and a book deal his agent had engineered with Random House. "Got a six-figure advance coming," he said between mouthfuls. It wasn't till she was serving ice cream and bakery pie for dessert that she realized he had asked her nothing about herself.

Gill did not volunteer to do dishes, but she asked him to wash and she would dry and put things away. He washed, but sloppily. She said nothing. He didn't seem accustomed to doing his own dishes. That meant a compliant girlfriend back in L.A.

After coffee, he sat on the couch and patted a place beside him, but she took a chair across the room. She hadn't imagined intimacy with him. After all, in the days of what they had called The Movement, people had crashed at any acquaintance's place without expecting to get laid. People shared what they had: food, clothing, a place to sleep. He had asked and she had agreed—to sleeping quarters, not necessarily to sleeping together.

He took out his toke bag and rolled a joint. A little uneasy at crossing to him, she let him bring it to her. She was staying off that couch unless she decided otherwise.

He leaned back lazily, grinning at her. He was tall and solidly built, with long medium blond hair in a ponytail. He no longer wore aviator glasses—probably, like herself, onto contact lenses. He radiated confidence and pleasure in himself. Well, she chided herself, he had done well without obvious compromise and did she want every man as neurotic as her ex-boyfriend Terry? Gill was even more attractive than he had been years ago.

"I have a gig at Madison starting in September," he said, his eyes fixed on hers. "Be there for a year. It's not that far, is it?"

Sheila shook her head. "Easy drive."

"I figure I'll be doing two classes and a seminar, so I could drive down weekends to Chicago . . ."

"It's surely doable, but you might enjoy Madison." She hoped he wasn't about to quiz her on the University or the town. She hadn't been there since the anti-war demonstrations.

"We've known each other for how many years?"

"Seven or eight, I'd say. Why?"

"And we've stayed in touch."

Occasional letters, a phone call or two, drinks together at conferences. "Off and on." Sheila forced a smile, wondering where this was leading. If he wanted to crash with her weekends, that would be a bit much. She wasn't running a B & B.

"I think it's inevitable . . . that we'll get involved. It's been moving that way for a long time." He patted the couch beside him again. "Inevitable."

She drew a sharp breath, flummoxed. It wasn't that she didn't have what she considered convenient sex. She still saw Terry sometimes. They had not broken up dramatically, just eased off and let it dwindle. But this guy lolling there on her couch telling her that she had no choice, it was just fate that she should have sex with him—she wanted to slug him. Choice was her bedrock belief about being a woman. She thought fast. "Gill, I have a boyfriend. A longtime thing. Pretty serious."

"Then where is he?"

"Off seeing his sister. She just had a miscarriage."

He looked around. "Does he live with you?"

She couldn't fake that. No male clothes, no shaving

equipment in the john. "We've tried that. Right now we're on different schedules so he has his own place."

"Is it an open relationship?" Still hopeful.

"That doesn't work for us. I don't have the time or energy."

He looked disgruntled. She understood he had thoroughly planned his coming academic year. Whoever was doing his dishes in L.A. was not accompanying him, so he had scheduled weekly bedtime with her in his photogenic head. Too bad.

In the morning, Gill took his stuff and left. Maybe he had a second somewhat less inevitable option on his to-do list.

Mid '90s

Amy was celebrating the primary victory of their candidate with the rest of the staff and a good number of volunteers. If Robin won, she would be the first woman senator from their state—ever. Amy believed in Robin with fervor. After all, she had written two of Robin's position papers prior to the debates, the one on abortion and contraception and the one on economic parity. Robin would fight for women and minorities and all the other causes Amy believed in.

There was Prosecco, beer, cookies, deviled eggs and an assortment of canapés donated from a restaurant that had quietly fed them several times during the campaign. Fortunately there were sodas, too. Amy didn't touch alcohol. Her father was a drunk who had beaten their mother, her older brother and occasionally her before he drove the family car into an overpass, killing himself and one of his drinking buddies.

Hardly anyone else abstained, although Robin confined herself to soda and nibbled sparingly of the hors d'oeuvres. But one other staff member too stayed off the booze—Brian, who was the point man on gun control and the environment.

"You don't drink. AA?"

"It's poison," he said. "I don't willingly pollute myself. We take in enough every time we breathe."

"Too true." She smiled. It felt as if they were the only two staid and sensible people in the room as the evening got rowdier. The press had come and gone before the party got going.

They stood together watching the room. He cleared his throat. "I've had enough celebrating ... Want to get a coffee? The fumes are getting to me."

"The coffee shop on the corner stays open till ten."

Quietly they slipped out into the mild September evening. Brian was a quiet sort, thin and trim with a bit of brown beard a shade lighter than his head hair, neatly trimmed. Everything about him was well kept—not fancy but clean, tidy. She liked that in a man. He wore button-down shirts and neat jeans. She knew he had some kind of job, so she asked them about it as they brought their cups to the table. He was drinking herb tea, she noticed. She had ordered decaf, in deference to the late hour she would get to bed this night.

"I'm a systems analyst."

She drew a blank. "What kind of systems?"

"I work with programming languages."

She guessed he didn't mean English or French. She had no idea what a computer language actually was, so she asked him. He explained. He explained some more. After a while she was only noticing his mouth was rather nicely full and his eyes were a sparkly blue behind his glasses and his fingers were long and shapely.

"You're a nurse practitioner." It was not a question.

She was startled that he had bothered to find out. Was something happening? She couldn't remember the last time she had been on a date. "Yes. I work in women's health."

"So how is that different from a regular nurse?"

"A couple of college degrees different." She paused, never

certain how much to explain. "I'm one step down from a 'real' doctor. I like it. We can get closer to patients and we're into prevention as much as cure."

That seemed to satisfy him. "I never understood how people like doctors and nurses who work with sick people keep from catching all those diseases."

"We wash our hands a lot." She smiled and he changed the subject.

During the next month, they had coffee, pizza together. Between her job and the campaign, she had little time to think about Brian, but she was comfortable with him. Obviously he was interested in her, but in no hurry to push things. She liked that. That was how things poked along until Robin lost the election to a vastly better funded campaign that flooded TV with ads depicting her as a someone who would raise taxes on everything in sight and turn the Commonwealth socialist.

For two weeks she did not see him, a bit depressed in the wake of a campaign into which she had put so much of herself. Then he called, asking her out for supper at an Indian restaurant. It was a low-key evening but pleasant. For the first time, he kissed her. She apologized for not asking him in, but she had a seminar early Saturday morning on new HIV medications and combinations.

The next weekend they spent the night together. He was an efficient lover, for someone had taught him to find the clitoris and use it. He was not passionate, but careful, considerate, patient. She was pleased. She'd had enough in her adolescence of men ramming themselves into her and banging away. She appreciated a man who thought of her pleasure as well as his own.

Sunday morning they rose late. She always had the Sunday *Times* delivered, but she would forgo it this morning for his company. She liked the way he looked tousled from bed, wearing her blue terry bathrobe after their mutual shower. I could get attached to him, she thought as she prepared French press coffee.

"None for me. I don't use stimulants."

She said mildly, "I doubt I could get through a day of patients without it. Medical personnel drink tons of coffee. It keeps us alert, and we have to be."

"I rely on meditation. I clear out the detritus from my mind, the same way I cleanse my colon."

She was not sure she wanted to know a great deal about his colon; in fact she was sure she did not. "Bacon and eggs? Or we could run out and get some croissants from the bakery in Davis Square."

"As a nurse, you should know that disease comes from impurities in the diet. I don't put anything you mentioned into my body. I avoid sugar, salt, animal fats and animal proteins of any kind. I'll take some tofu and rice milk."

"I don't have any . . ."

"I'll bring some next time I sleep over. I'll bring enough for you." He looked at her carefully. "I see your eyes are a bit bloodshot. Too much stimulant. You have to cut back."

He rose, took her coffee cup and spilled her lovely French roast into the sink. She sat with her mouth slightly open in shock.

He beamed at her. "You need to be far more aware what you consume. I also recommend a juice fast every two weeks. I'm surprised you aren't more careful and it makes me wonder what kind of prevention you recommend to your patients. I can help you." He took her hand. "And I want to. You're basically a good person, but you have bad habits."

"Well, if you won't eat anything I have, I hope you won't mind if I . . ." she was about to say 'fry' but thought better, "poach myself a couple of eggs."

"Please don't. As a vegan, I grow ill if I have to inhale the scent of animal protein."

She wanted to ask how he had endured the pizza parlor, then, or the campaign office where half the volunteers were chowing down on hamburgers or sandwiches. "What would you like to do this morning?"

"I brought my running shoes. Why don't we go to Fresh Pond Reservoir?"

She poured herself a bowl of cereal. He picked up the cereal box and began reading out the ingredients. She interrupted the recital. "I don't think I'm up for a run this morning. I may be coming down with a cold." And if I'm near the reservoir, I might not be able to resist pushing you in. She ignored his lecture on the herbs she should be imbibing as she headed for the bathroom. Maybe when she came out, he would be gone. Permanently.

Mid Oughts

Jessie met Aidan at one of those flash dating lunches where she sat at a table and a bevy of men passed through one at a time for two minutes each. Her impression of him, fleeting certainly, was that Aidan was unusually polite and put together. He was one of only two of the prospective dates she filled out a card saying she'd see again. The other one never called.

Jessie had worked at a battered women's shelter until she burned out. She could not even contemplate associating intimately with a man for a couple of years afterward, when she had gone back to school and gotten a Masters in social work. In her job for an agency that handled foster children, she worked in an office full of women of all ages and races. When she finally decided it was time to look for male companionship, she had no idea where to start till one of the married women in the office recommended this online site where she could sign up. It sounded benign enough, just two minutes with a guy and no dangerous contact or information given. She had to eat lunch anyhow.

Aiden and she met for their first date in a restaurant in midtown mostly popular with younger and more affluent customers. He was already waiting when she arrived, nicely got up in a navy blazer and neat khakis, a shirt checked in pale blue. He had short blond hair she remembered and attractive glasses. Behind them his eyes were hazel with rather long lashes for a man. His hands gripping the menu looked manicured. She felt conscious of her own that were not. She couldn't remember ever having her nails done, although some of the younger women in her office sported multicolored talons.

He ordered a steak; she ordered a Cobb salad that almost fit into her budget. They each had a glass of wine, making small talk about the weather, the Yankees, although she herself preferred that underdog perennially heartbreaking team, the Mets. They exchanged information on their families. Both of them came from similar backgrounds, she was pleased to note: she had been born in Jersey, in East Orange. He was from Hicksville on Long Island. They had both intended from early adolescence to move into the city. Her father was an insurance salesman, not a very successful one. Her mother, when she and her brother were old enough, worked as a receptionist in a doctor's office. His father had a shoe store that went broke and his mother was a nurse in pediatrics. He had one sister; she had one brother, both younger than themselves. She began to feel this might go somewhere.

She explained her job. He commented, "Can't be much money in that."

"A lot more than where I worked before, in a battered women's shelter."

Silence.

"What do you do?"

He was in derivatives. The more he explained, the less she understood. Finally she decided to change the subject.

"How do you see yourself say in five years? Your goals . . ." It felt a bit formal, as if she were interviewing him for a job.

He liked that question. "I want to move up at Stepler and Coakes. I drive a BMW but I want something . . . finer. A Lamborghini really says success. I've bought a condo in the Back Bay, but I want a water view, not the alley behind." It was as if he had lit up from within. His face was suddenly animated. He removed his glasses and his eyes shone. "I'd like a house in the Caribbean to take a winter vacation where it's warm. I rent a place for two weeks in January, but it's pretty primitive—just three rooms half a mile from the beach in Santa Lucia, although it does come with maid service. But you can't leave anything lying around, of course . . . A wife, I guess." He nodded at her. "Kids, eventually. But the main thing is to move up and get the lifestyle. I've been accepted into a couple of useful clubs, but until I do better, I can't move up there either. If I'd gone to Harvard . . . I did go to Harvard Business School, of course, but I don't have the connections those dudes who came up through prep schools and then Harvard have to ease their way . . ."

Jessie slept alone that night, as always. She decided that two minutes was not nearly enough to get a fix on someone.

Recently

"But I thought girls were into vampires."

"My wife was a real bitch. She kept trying to pussywhip me and tie an apron around my balls."

"Those girls who walk around in low cut tops and short skirts are just asking for it."

"I bet Hillary has fat thighs and stretch marks."

"So I got fired just for watching porn at the office."

"Why don't you sext me some hot photos of you touching yourself?"

"But we're separated and I'll be getting a divorce any day now."

"I'm into Scientology ... The Fundamentalist Church of Utter Humiliation for Women ... The Flat Earth Society ... New Creationism ... The Tea Party ... The Illuminati ... The KKK ... etc." The list keeps growing as does stupidity.

Any Old Time

When Rachel met Seth, he invited her over for supper. He cooked a delicious chicken cacciatore, put on an apron and washed the dishes afterward. He was considerate and knowledgeable in bed. He consulted her before making mutual dates or appointments. When she spoke, he actually listened. His politics were fine.

Of course after they moved in together, she learned that chicken cacciatore was one of the only three dishes he knew how to cook, but to this day, he puts on an apron and does the dishes. He still listens when she speaks. She is happy she met him.

The Secret of My Marriage

I grew up with my mother as head of our family—our father died when I was a toddler. I never knew much about his family except that they had moved far away to the land of Canaan. My uncle was supposedly in charge, but my mother has always been a strong woman and she raised us pretty much on her own. We were neither poor nor rich. We had a flock of thirty-one sheep, two cows, and three goats. My brothers took care of the animals, Mother sold food from a stall in the market, and I ran the house.

I was of marrying age, but no one appropriate had appeared. Mother was beginning to show her age. I worried for her and for our family, always looking for some way to give us security. I had to marry well, I knew that, although I didn't much look forward to my bride price being paid for some old tyrant who'd beat me or drive me crazy with jealousy. I kept my eye out for someone likely. But the wealthier families had no interest in ours and the poorer ones basically wanted a female slave to produce workers and toil in the fields. We had little land, a small flock and too many brothers. I'm viewed as pretty, but that counts for little in marrying in our village. Men gaze at me when I am carrying water to and from the well, but their gazes are lustful, not useful.

It was late afternoon when I went to fetch water from the village well, as I did every morning and again just before I fixed the evening meal. A strange man was hanging around the well, not a beggar obviously. He had servants and a pack train of camels. Yet he was not dressed like a wealthy man himself, in respectable clothes although dusty from traveling. He asked me to draw him some water from the well for his thirst.

Now, he could very well have drawn some himself, so I paused to consider why he was asking me. I decided it might be some sort of test. Even though I was tired and had still to make our meal, I drew water for him and then for his camels and servants. He was watching me with a judgmental eye and I was sure I had guessed right. He seemed satisfied with me. He prayed for a moment. Then he pressed upon me gold jewelry, a nose ring, and two bracelets. I could feel they were solid gold. He insisted I put them on. I obliged, trying to guess how much we could get for them in the market. I congratulated myself on drawing all that water.

Now I was late so I made to leave, balancing my jar on my head. The stranger asked if perhaps my father could put him up for the night. I explained that Father had passed on, but that we could easily take care of him and his servants and camels. "Who is your family?" He asked.

When I answered, he got visibly excited and exclaimed to his god his good fortune. He announced himself as the servant of a kinsman, one of those in the family who had gone so far away. Obviously they had done well for themselves. I showed my new golden jewelry to my brothers and my oldest brother Laban went running to greet the man and bring him inside and lavish him with what hospitality we had. I hung back, observing. The servant announced that we were his goal. I wondered what our relatives in Canaan wanted—what did they have in mind, sending this servant and his caravan in search of us. We settled the man and his entourage and camels in for the night. We slaughtered one of our lambs and I prepared a feast. Mother came home from the market and when she saw the bracelets, she changed into her best clothes and brought out our good wine.

But the stranger would not eat what we had laid out so lavishly, using the last of our spices. He insisted he must explain something first. He went on about the good fortune of his master, the son of Avram whom he called Abraham, and the son of his old age upon whom even greater good fortune had fallen. He had been sent to find a bride for his master's son. I asked very quietly and modestly, with my eyes cast down, how old was this son.

"Forty years this season," the stranger said.

Forty years old and his father takes charge of finding him a wife. Why wait so long for a helpmate? This was not a powerful man but the son of a powerful father. I asked how old was the man who now called himself Abraham. Well over a hundred. So we have a powerful father in his extreme old age and a weak son. The father could not possibly live a lot longer. The mother, called Sarah, had died relatively recently. I listened and I heard a situation where I might have some authority myself.

The stranger brought out a great heap of presents— mostly gold and silver—that he piled in front of me, gave to my mother, to Laban, to my other brothers. Everyone's eyes were huge and they practically fell on their knees to the man. Of course, of course I should be married to this man, Isaac he was called. So everyone feasted and then slept.

In the morning, the man wanted to be off to his master and his master's son with me, but my family was hesitant now to send me off into who knew what situation. Finally they left it up to me. I said at once, "I will," for I was sure of my estimate of the situation and ready to pick up and go.

There was nothing for me here except drudgery into old age. I was ready to take my chances with this forty-year-old Isaac.

We traveled and traveled. I got little out of the servant with my probing, no matter how subtle. At last we arrived and I could see at once the servant had not exaggerated: these relatives of ours were indeed well off. I was presented first to Abraham in his large and well-appointed tent where I knelt on the beautiful carpet before him. He asked me many questions about my family. I kept my eyes modestly downcast and answered in a soft sweet voice. I had no intention of being sent back. Finally he seemed satisfied and sent the servant to fetch Isaac. Isaac was a shy, slightly awkward man, tall and lean and more boyish than likely for a man of his age. In his father's shadow, indeed. It was difficult for him to look at me, so I boldly took his hand. Then our eyes met and I knew I had him.

We were married quickly, as if Abraham were afraid I would disappear or something would go wrong. When we were alone, I cast off my veil and smiled at my new husband. "Don't be afraid," I murmured in his ear and seduced him gently. He trembled when I touched him. Although I was of course a virgin, my mother had long ago explained the ways of men and women to me and I'd watched the sheep and goats. It was like taming a lamb, getting him to trust me. He missed his mother all the time, because she had always tried to protect him from his father. He wept and I held him, like his mother, he said.

"I will keep you safe better than your mother could," I promised, "for she owed obedience to her husband but my first loyalty is to you." I wondered what caused him to be so fearful. The family had no enemies I could see.

He put his head in my lap and fell asleep.

One night he told me about his miserable childhood, when his father had been ready to kill him on a high mountain, laying him down on a rock like lamb to be sacrificed and brandishing a terrible long knife over him. Since that time, he lived in fear of his father, afraid the man might take it upon himself to finish the job. Abraham had also sent away his other son into the desert, exiling him without mercy because of some disrespect his mother, a handmaiden, had shown Sarah. From then on I understood Isaac's weakness and whenever possible I took his side, lying when necessary, taking any blame on myself. Under my protection, he grew less tentative, less withdrawn. After his father finally died, I gave Isaac two sons. It was I who ruled in the house of Abraham and Isaac was content.

What Is the Meaning of This?

It was in the mid '70s, and I was in what we called then an open relationship. That meant my husband Brad fucked any young woman he could get his hands on and I had a few long-term relationships that usually fell apart when it became apparent I wasn't going to leave my husband. Brad and I had been together since college and I found it hard to envision life without him. I was an assistant professor of English at Hunter, hired as a Virginia Woolf scholar— I'd published two books on her, the second with a New York press since interest in her had taken off. I received a modest advance and the book lingered for a while. Still, an increasing number of universities had women's studies departments; now and then I gave a lecture or took part in a conference or seminar on Woolf. I had visited Sissinghurst to do some research there on a Guggenheim and had a brief affair with her grandson, who lived in the house among the still wonderful gardens.

I was giving a talk at Smith. Often when I do those gigs, the faculty takes me out to dinner, usually with a couple of the brightest students. This time we were eating at a Japanese restaurant in Northampton. The chair of the

English Department was across the table, ignoring me to flirt with a young man beside him. On my right was the resident Woolf scholar who was attempting to prove errors of commission and omission in my published work. On my left was a graduate student I noticed managed to push aside two others to take that place.

She introduced herself as Sonia Whittaker. Sonia made intense eye contact whenever I looked her way, which was fairly often since I longed to escape the attacks of the woman on my right. Sonia was not beautiful for there was something too sharp in her features, but she was attractive. She was a honey blonde with large, changeable green eyes, cat's eyes flecked with gold. High cheekbones. She wore her hair short and affected green nails and long dangly earrings. Her cleavage peeked out of a silk blouse with several buttons undone.

She flirted with me. I wasn't used to that. I'm not much of a flirt, but I was flattered. "I'm such a fan of your work," she said in a breathy voice. "You're so brilliant, I wish I was your student."

"You're interested in Virginia Woolf?"

"I'd be interested in anything you write about."

I was scheduled to give a seminar in the late afternoon before driving home to Brooklyn. She showed up at breakfast at the dorm where they had me stashed and offered to show me around. I ate eggs; she drank black coffee.

"I loved *Among the Tweenies*," she breathed. I was shocked by the compliment. I published an obscure book of short stories with a tiny feminist press a couple of years before. Brad called it the Three Witches Press, and found it amusing. I can't exaggerate how exciting it was to hear that somebody had actually read and liked it. She commented on several of the stories, which made me want to dance across the ceiling. I'd had some good reviews, but only 1,104 copies had sold, mostly to libraries. Meeting a fan was a rare experience.

"Truly, I could envy you. Such a brilliant academic reputation, already on the tenure track, invited to speak at so many universities—and then a magnificent talent for stories."

"It's just one book. I don't know if I'll ever do it again. I don't know if I can."

"You have a rare sensibility. It makes me want to know you better." She took my hand in hers. How warm it was. "What are you doing next weekend?" Her index finger drew circles on my hand. My breath turned solid in my throat. "I know you live in New York. I could easily drive."

She read my expression of doubt and added, "I'm older than you probably think. Twenty-six. I worked in publishing for a few years before going back to school." Much later, I learned she had temped at Harcourt Brace one summer and that she was thirty.

Brad and I shared a house with another couple up the Hudson in Cold Spring and drove or took the train there Friday night returning Sunday. Our three-room apartment in Brooklyn Heights was small and noisy in spite of the high rent, but Brad liked the address. I never could write there. We tripped over each other. We were forced to share our neighbors' taste in music and to listen to the couple downstairs fighting about money. It was always a great relief to get away. In the nineteenth-century house in Cold Spring, I had my own study and so did Brad. We occupied the whole second floor. He was a TV personality with an interview show just after the news on Channel 4. Syndication was being discussed. He made much more money than I did. I was used to being ignored when I went to parties with him.

I explained my situation, the open relationship, the tiny apartment, the lovely big house we shared in Cold Spring. Her finger was still traveling around my palm, making its sensual way between my fingers. Was she coming on to me? I had never had an affair with a woman, although half my female friends had announced themselves lesbians in the past couple of years. They were always pushing me to try women, so that maybe I would leave Brad.

"I could come out the weekend after this. Would you like that?"

"Sure," I said. She leaned across the table and kissed me briefly, a brush of her lips against mine. Then she rose. "I'm so looking forward to getting to know you really well."

I was flustered and confused. Perhaps I was about to be initiated into a club to which so many of my friends belonged. It was flattering; it was nervous-making. Would I know what to do? I felt as if I should read a book on the subject to prepare. I hadn't been involved with anyone besides Brad for more than ten months. Relationships did not come easily to me; none I'd had were what you'd call casual. I did not know what to expect and in the interim, I was often tempted to call the visit off. But Brad encouraged me.

"Sounds like fun. Why not try something with a woman, especially if she's as attractive as you say. It'd be good for you. You've been romancing books instead of partners for months." He grinned. "Why not? A change would perk you up."

I felt a bit pushed. "I didn't think I needed perking."

"You've been in a bit of a rut." I thought about how often he found little ways to announce his superiority, but I kept quiet. Of course Brad was not only more famous than I could ever imagine I'd be, but he was six feet two, perhaps a bit heavier than when we married, with a firm chin, tea-colored hair the studio arranged for upkeep, striking light blue almost silver eyes. I'd had a crush on him for six months before he noticed me—we shared a sociology class and I gave him my notes. Soon he leaned on me for help with all his classes. I wrote a few of his papers.

I decided I'd let things with Sonia take their course. She arrived Friday night just before ten. I had taught three courses that day with a couple of student conferences in between. I'd then cooked a supper of beef stroganoff, rice, and a salad. Brad made drinks and we three chatted about the weather, Cold Spring, Smith, television, recent art movies. By eleven thirty I was nodding out. I had no idea what to expect, but I couldn't stay awake longer. Perhaps she could follow me to my room. When I made my excuses, having pointed out my bedroom when I was settling her in the guest room, she was still questioning Brad about what it is like to interview celebrities.

I tried to stay awake in case she came to me, but I was exhausted and slept. I got up once during the night but I did not see her and assumed she was sleeping in the guest room. I was a little relieved. It gave me time to get to know her better. I had never been intimate with anyone I knew so little about.

In the morning I woke at eight. I could smell coffee. One of Brad's sweet habits was making café au lait in the mornings. I got myself up, combed my hair, put on my flannel bathrobe, and headed for the kitchen. I was surprised to see Sonia at the table already, in a black dressing gown with a lacy black negligee peeking out. Brad was telling a story that Sonia was listening to with rapt attention, leaning forward in a way that increased her décolletage. Brad was bustling about the kitchen apparently making an omelet with bits of parsley from a pot I kept on the window ledge. Usually he didn't make breakfast; usually I did. Not that I minded being cooked for, but everything struck me as a little off.

While we were finishing breakfast, he said, "By the way, I'm taking Sonia to the city today. She wanted to see the setup at the studio, and I have a little work to do on my next interview."

It all fell into place. Where Sonia had slept. Why Brad was being so nice at breakfast. For a moment I felt like crying. I'd thought for once someone was actually more interested in me than in my husband.

I felt brave as I said, "I shouldn't expect you back then this evening. I imagine you'll stay in Brooklyn."

"At the Heights brownstone, most likely."

Sonia beamed at me. "I know you must have work too, prepping for class and all. See you tomorrow back here."

"Perhaps," I said, controlling my face. I stopped being sorry for myself and began to be quietly angry. At both of them. A stepping stone, me. He couldn't let me have one tiny illusion, one ego-swelling flirtation? How many of my women friends had he enjoyed brief affairs with, leaving my own relationship with them somehow lessened. And when he dumped them, I was always to blame.

I held it together and in fact had work to do for the week's classes. When Brad returned alone Sunday afternoon, I was surprised but glad Sonia was not with him. He said she'd driven back to Northampton.

"Did it not go as well as you expected?"

He grimaced. "One of those women who think because I screw them a couple of times, they can get a job at the station. They must think I'm incredibly naïve. That's no basis for a hire, ever."

"I imagine that's what she came here for."

"Of course." He chuckled. "You thought she was coming on to you. You've never been great at picking up clues."

"Guess not," I said. I think it was at that moment I decided that I was going to leave him. It would take a while to work out the details, but as suddenly as it came upon me, I was quite, quite sure. And I did so six weeks later, with the help of the very best divorce lawyer I could find. Brad was incredulous, then furious. Sonia called me three weeks after her visit. I hung up.

ABOUT PM PRESS

PM Press was founded at the end of 2007 by a small collection of folks with decades of publishing, media, and organizing experience. PM Press co-conspirators have published and distributed hundreds of books, pamphlets, CDs, and DVDs. Members of PM have founded enduring book fairs, spearheaded victorious tenant organizing campaigns, and worked closely with bookstores, academic conferences, and even rock bands to deliver political and challenging ideas to all walks of life. We're old enough to know what we're doing and young enough to know what's at stake. PM Press is always on the lookout for talented and skilled volunteers, artists, activists and writers to work with. If you have a great idea for a project or can contribute in some way, please get in touch.

PM Press, PO Box 23912, Oakland, CA 94623 www.pmpress.org

FRIENDS OF PM PRESS

These are indisputably momentous times—the financial system is melting down globally and the Empire is stumbling. Now more than ever there is a vital need for radical ideas. *Friends of PM* allows you to directly help impact, amplify, and revitalize the discourse and actions of radical writers, filmmakers, and artists. It provides us with a stable foundation from which we can build upon our early successes and provides a much-needed subsidy for the materials that can't necessarily pay their own way. You can help make that happen—and receive every new title automatically delivered to your door once a month—by joining as a Friend of PM Press. And, we'll throw in a free T-shirt when you sign up.

Here are your options:

- **$30 a month** Get all books and pamphlets plus 50% discount on all webstore purchases

- **$40 a month** Get all PM Press releases (including CDs and DVDs) plus 50% discount on all webstore purchases

- **$100 a month** Superstar—Everything plus PM merchandise, free downloads, and 50% discount on all webstore purchases

For those who can't afford $30 or more a month, we're introducing **Sustainer Rates** at $15, $10 and $5. Sustainers get a free PM Press T-shirt and a 50% discount on all purchases from our website.

Your Visa or Mastercard will be billed once a month, until you tell us to stop. Or until our efforts succeed in bringing the revolution around. Or the financial meltdown of Capital makes plastic redundant. Whichever comes first.

Braided Lives

Marge Piercy

ISBN: 978-1-60486-442-7
$20.00   456 pages

Marge Piercy carries her portrait of
the American experience back into the
Fifties—that closed, repressive time
in which forces for the upheavals of
the Sixties ticked away underground.
Spanning twenty years, and teeming
with vivid characters, *Braided Lives* tells
the powerful, unsentimental story of
two young women coming of age.

Braided Lives is an enduring portrait of the past that has led to our
tenuous present.

Vida

Marge Piercy

ISBN: 978-1-60486-487-8
$20.00   416 pages

Originally published in 1979, *Vida*
is Marge Piercy's classic bookend
to the Sixties. At the center of the
novel stands Vida Asch. She has
lived underground for almost a
decade. Back in the Sixties she was
a political star of the exuberant
antiwar movement but now, a
decade later, Vida is on the run. Piercy's characters make vivid and
comprehensible the desperation, the courage, and the blind rage of
a time when "action" could appear to some to be a more rational
choice than the vote.

Dance the Eagle to Sleep: A Novel

Marge Piercy

ISBN: 978-1-60486-456-4
$17.95   208 pages

Originally published in 1970, Marge Piercy's second novel follows the lives of four teenagers, in a near future society, as they rebel against a military draft and "the system." The occupation of Franklin High School begins, and with it, the open rebellion of America's youth against their channeled, unrewarding lives and the self-serving, plastic society that directs them. This is a future fiction without a drop of fantasy.

My Life, My Body

Marge Piercy

ISBN: 978-1-62963-105-9
$12.00   128 pages

In a candid and intimate new collection of essays, poems, memoirs, reviews, rants, and railleries, Piercy discusses her own development as a working-class feminist, the highs and lows of TV culture, the ego-dances of a writer's life, the homeless and the housewife, Allen Ginsberg and Marilyn Monroe, feminist utopias (and why she doesn't live in one), why fiction isn't physics; and of course, fame, sex, and money, not necessarily in that order. The short essays, poems, and personal memoirs intermingle like shards of glass that shine, reflect—and cut. Always personal yet always political, Piercy's work is drawn from a deep well of feminist and political activism.

Also featured is our Outspoken Interview, in which the author lays out her personal rules for living on Cape Cod, finding your poetic voice, and making friends in Cuba.